AF409558

Murder in the Fawnwood Museum

A Gallery Cafe Mystery

Sydney Tate

CAR Publishing

Copyright © 2023 by Sydney Tate

All rights reserved.

No portion of this book may be reproduced in any form without written permission from the publisher or author, except as permitted by U.S. copyright law.

Contents

Chapter 1

The Gallery Café buzzed with anticipation as we prepared to cater the Fawnwood Museum's masquerade ball, unaware that the evening's theme of "Mystery and Intrigue" would become all too real. The Fawnwood Museum's masquerade ball was an event we all looked forward to, but this year, the masks would serve as more than just decorative attire–they would conceal a deadly secret.

My rabbit Tetley, with his soft white fur and always-twitching nose, watched lazily from his bed in the corner of the dining area, nibbling on a carrot stick in his hutch. "And just what do you think you're up to, fuzzy friend?" Tetley twitched his nose in faux innocence, as if he hadn't already devised a scheme to pilfer treats the moment I turned my back.

"Lola, do you need help with those cream puffs?" asked my best friend Polly, tying an apron around her waist. "Or maybe we could make some hors d'oeuvres inspired by famous paintings? Imagine a mini Starry Night quiche or a Mona Lisa canapé!" We both giggled at the thought. Her short blonde hair was styled in its usual pixie cut. As an artist, Polly dressed in her signature quirky style - today it was pink cropped pants, an oversized lime green sweater and chunky beaded necklaces.

"Help would be wonderful. Thanks Polly. But let's stick to basic pastries. The event planner just called and said they're expecting even more people than they'd originally thought. At this rate, we'll be catering for the whole town!" I said, wiping a stray hair from my forehead. I surveyed the trays surrounding me, filled with days of work and worrying if it would all pay off. The museum had spared no expense for this event, but my café's finances were fragile. I needed this catering job to go off without a hitch.

The Fawnwood Museum had always been a beacon of art and culture in our small town, and when they contacted me to cater their upcoming masquerade ball, I was thrilled. It was the museum's annual fundraising event, and this year they were unveiling a new art collection. The theme was "Mystery and Intrigue." For the occasion, the event planner suggested something unusual: instead of our usual Gallery Café jacket uniforms, Polly and I would don masks to match the guests. The idea was to add a touch of fun and flair to our catering service, fully embracing the theme of the evening. We agreed, excited to be part of the grand spectacle.

A couple hours later, Polly and I arrived at the museum, directing staff to set up under the intricate molding and glittering chandeliers of the ballroom. Golden masks, feathers and beads adorned every surface, with servers in vests and bow ties already serving champagne to elaborately dressed guests.

The museum's exhibits featured massive abstract sculptures, disorienting neon installations, and an eerie silent film on loop. In the Modern Art gallery, something about the flicker of the antique projector gave me chills—a strange sense of foreboding I couldn't place.

"This is so lavish," Polly whispered to me, adjusting the mask on her face, her blonde pixie cut just visible around the edges. I nodded, though my mask made it difficult. I caught a glimpse of the museum's director, Mr. Worthington, greeting guests by the entrance. He was taking the event very seriously, his aged face stern as always. I noticed him engaging in a tense conversation with a masked figure, their words barely audible amidst the din.

"...no, no ... we had an agreement! I won't accept this," Mr. Worthington said.

"You'll get your payment when our work is done. Do not forget who is in charge here!" the masked figure replied.

I whispered to Polly, "What do you think that's about? Mr. Worthington looks quite upset."

Polly frowned, leaning in close. "I don't know, but I have a bad feeling about it. That masked guy did not look friendly."

As Polly and I were circulating during the event, Mr. Worthington flagged us down, an irritated look on his face. "You there, caterer! This champagne has gone warm. Have someone bring me a properly chilled glass this instant!"

I rushed over, putting on my most professional smile. "Right away, sir. My apologies." As I walked off to find a replacement flute of champagne, I rolled my eyes at Polly. The audacity of that man, as if catering this lavish gala wasn't difficult enough!

I returned with his drink and courteously handed it to him. "Here you are, sir. Enjoy the rest of the evening." I suppressed my annoyance and focused on providing the best service possible.

As the evening progressed, Polly and I made the rounds, refilling trays and ensuring all the guests were happy. A quartet played classical music in the corner, just audible over the din of laughter and chatter.

The ornate clocks chimed eleven, and guests began spilling into the museum's exhibit halls for the unveiling of the new art collection.

In the Modern Art gallery, a scream rang out, shattering the revelry into chaos. Polly and I rushed over to find a crowd gathering around one of the interactive sculptures—and Mr. Worthington lying motionless at its base, eyes frozen wide in an eternal stare. A look of utter shock on his face, as a pool of deep red seeped onto the stark white floor around him.

Amongst the gilded masks and elaborate gowns at the Fawnwood Museum's masquerade ball, the line between fantasy and reality had blurred—with fatal consequences.

Chaos erupted as panic spread like wildfire through the hall. Guests shoved and shouted, rushing for exits in a frenzied evacuation. In their haste, a woman lost her shoe, the heel snapping off. A man tore his coat on the jagged edge of a sculpture. Polly fought against the tide of silk and taffeta to reach my side. Word of the grim discovery spread like wildfire through the museum halls.

"Lola! Are you alright?" Polly grasped my arm, eyes wide with fear beneath her golden mask. "How did this happen?"

I shook my head, too stunned to do more than stare at the horror unfolding before us.

In the distance, a familiar voice rang out. "Make way, police!"

My heart leaped as Detective Harry pushed through the crowd, flanked by uniformed officers. His gaze met mine, eyes softening briefly before taking in the grim scene.

He crouched down beside Mr. Worthington's body, carefully examining the surroundings before straightening up and addressing his team. "Secure the area and start taking statements. We need to find out who was close to the victim when this happened." As he scanned the room, he caught my eyes, allowing a small, reassuring smile to break through his professional demeanor. His brown eyes locked onto mine, and a flush rose to my cheeks at the familiar mischievous glint there—even now.

I knew I could trust Harry to sort this out, yet our usual flirtatious rapport added tension to the situation. As he moved through the crowd, I found myself unable to look away, captivated by the calm confidence of his movements and quick, cunning questions—though a killer was in our midst. For a moment, the chaos faded and there was only the detective, brow furrowed in thought...

We gave shaken statements about discovering the body and spotting no clear culprit in the frenzied evacuation. The museum was cordoned off, pending a full investigation, sequins and feathers littering the steps as lingering traces of the merriment which had descended into murder dissipated.

Polly insisted on brewing strong cups of tea back at our apartment once we were released. "Quite a disastrous first public event, wouldn't you say?" Her wry humor did little to mask the haunted look in her eyes.

I nodded, clutching my cup for warmth as worry set in. "Between the museum's grand reopening and this new art collection, the board will be devastated. And if word gets out about the murder, it may ruin our café's reputation by association, too." My stomach churned at how swiftly our fortunes had unraveled.

"We can't just sit idle while a killer escapes and our livelihood crumbles." Polly's eyes glinted with fierce determination. I knew that glint well—my free-spirited friend had the bit between her teeth. There would be no deterring her from investigating this case, and truth be told, my curiosity was piqued. We were in this together, come what may, and we had a secret weapon on our side ... if I could persuade a certain dashing detective to accept our help.

The next morning, Polly and I began canvassing the neighborhood around the museum, hoping to find clues the police may have overlooked. We started with the antiquarian bookseller next door, who often took tea at the café.

"There were so many costumed guests, I couldn't claim to know them all," he said apologetically. "But I overheard a heated exchange between Mr. Worthington and a tall gentleman in a top hat."

Another argument? This guy had definitely not been making many new friends on the night of his death.

Polly and I exchanged looks, intrigued by this piece of gossip. "Were you able to glean what the argument was about?" I pressed gently.

The bookseller shook his head. "I'm afraid they moved out of earshot. But Mr. Worthington seemed quite agitated."

We thanked him for the information and continued down the street, pondering this recent development. If Worthington had quarreled with someone, it may point to another suspect—or perhaps even a motive.

A florist we frequented for the café had noticed nothing amiss, nor had a grocer we often purchased spices and teas from. We were feeling discouraged as we headed back to the café when Polly picked up her pace upon spotting a glittering object caught in a grate by the museum steps.

"Look, Lola—a mask." She reached down and carefully extracted a golden half mask set with shimmering crystals and feathers. "Someone dropped this when leaving last night."

It was just like all the other masks that had been lost in the chaos, but as I examined the mask, I noticed a tiny compartment in the frame.

Curious, I pried it open to reveal a small, ancient-looking key. Polly and I exchanged puzzled glances. Why would someone hide a key in a mask, and what did it unlock?

The key was intricately designed, with strange symbols etched into its surface. This wasn't just an ordinary key. The symbols seemed to be of a language long forgotten, or perhaps purposely hidden.

Polly furrowed her brow, concern etched on her face. "If the killer hid this key so carefully, it must unlock something important. What if they notice it's missing and come after us?"

Her eyes widened at the thought. I placed a reassuring hand on her arm.

"Don't worry. We'll be careful," I grinned. "And anyway, unless you put a lost and found 'ad' in the newspaper or post signs around town, how would anyone know we have this key?"

Polly nodded, though she still seemed on edge. I tried again to ease the tension with humor. "At least all those detective shows we watch are finally proving useful! We'll solve this before things get danger-ous."

Polly laughed softly. "I hope you're right. But this killer was daring enough to strike in public. We can't take any chances."

"Maybe we should leave the rest of the sleuthing to the police," Polly suggested. "I don't want us getting in over our heads, no matter how exciting this is."

I hesitated, part of me longing to unlock the mysteries this key seemed to hold, yet dreading what it might reveal. "You make a good point. Let's see what clues the key itself provides first before going any further."

Chapter 2

In the morning, the old radio hummed gently in the corner of our cozy kitchen, a familiar comfort I struggled to tune in. My thoughts were consumed by the disquieting memories of the masquerade ball and its tragic aftermath. Mr. Worthington's pale, lifeless face. The ornate key we had found, holding untold secrets. At least, I thought, Tetley hadn't sneaked in and caused his own brand of chaos at the ball.

"We have to go back." Polly stood by the counter, clutching a mug of coffee as though it were a lifeline. Her pixie cut stuck out at odd angles, blonde strands catching the golden morning light filtering through the curtains. But her eyes were alert, sharp with determination. "I bet that key unlocks something in the museum. We need to find out what a killer might have wanted it for."

I nodded, determination outweighing the fear churning in my stomach.

The doors were unlocked, but the museum was eerily silent, police tape still cordoning off sections. We wandered through the Modern Art gallery where the body had been found, searching for any clues the police may have missed.

As we examined the interactive sculpture Worthington had been standing by before his death, Polly jokingly asked, "Do you think the sculpture was called 'Mystery and Intrigue' because nobody knows what it's supposed to be?"

Just as I was about to respond, a voice called out to us. "I apologize, but the museum is still closed for investigation."

We turned to see a handsome guard approaching, footsteps echoing on the marble floor. He was tall and broad shouldered, with wind-tousled dark hair and piercing blue eyes. His uniform did little to conceal a toned, athletic physique. His name tag read 'Jake'.

Polly flashed him her most charming smile. "We're friends of Mr. Worthington. Just hoping to find closure. I'm Polly and this is Lola. We own the Gallery Café."

Jake's expression softened. "My condolences. I'm Jake, one of the night guards. I was actually off duty on the night of the ball, an unexpected family emergency..." He shook our hands, pausing as his eyes fell on the key in my palm. "Where did you get that?"

I hesitated. Could we trust this stranger, no matter how disarming his smile was?

Sensing my discomfort, Jake continued, "I've worked here for years, and I've never seen a key like that. But some of these old exhibits have hidden compartments that might need specialized keys. I could show you around, see if it fits anywhere?"

Polly and I exchanged glances. This could be our chance to uncover the key's secrets, even if it meant deceiving the guard. I slipped the key into my pocket and smiled. "A tour would be lovely, thanks."

As Jake showed us through dusty storage rooms and behind locked doors, I studied his finely chiseled features, trying to read his intent. His knowledge of the building's secret spaces was uncanny. Was he helping us out of kindness, or manipulating us for his own unknown ends? I couldn't help but think that he, too, would have made quite an impression at the masquerade ball with his natural air of mystery.

"My family has had a long, complicated history with the Worthingtons and this museum," Jake admitted, noting my quizzical look. "I took this job to get closer to the truth of what happened here years ago. You see, I am a DuPont. My mother is the daughter of Elias DuPont. And, well, I've always had a thing for antique keys and secret compartments." He let out a wry laugh, then nodded at me. "When I saw you had that key, I thought maybe you were caught up in the same web of secrets I've been trying to untangle. And I think I might know what that key goes to."

He led us to a storage area in the east wing, filled with artifacts not currently on display. The dim lighting cast a roguish glow on his chiseled features, emphasizing the air of mystery that seemed to surround him. "This key looks quite old. My guess is it unlocks something in one of these older collections."

With surprising ease, he moved aside a heavy crate to reveal a wooden door with an ornate lock. "This leads to our antique weapons vault. Not even the police have searched in there yet. The door mechanism is tamper-proof, so no one could just break in, and it needs a specific key..."

As he spoke, the passion in his voice grew palpable, as if the museum's secrets were intertwined with his own. "Can I see that key for a moment?" He slid the key easily into the lock. When he turned the key, we could hear the lock clicking open with a loud 'thunk'. With a twist of the knob and a great heave, the heavy door creaked open, revealing a room filled with ancient swords, maces, and shields. Glass cases held daggers, throwing stars, and pistols from centuries past.

I noticed something peculiar—one display case was empty. "Looks like something's missing," I murmured, thinking how even this room seemed to have its own masquerade going on, with empty cases hiding their true purpose.

Jake's blue eyes scanned the room, their intensity betraying his concern. "You're right. We documented every item in this collection. I need to report this to the police right away." His voice held a hint of panic.

As Jake turned away to talk on the radio, I noticed a glint of gold under one of the cabinets. Reaching down, I pulled out an intricately carved dagger and gasped—the hilt was covered in blood.

Polly's eyes widened, and she barely whispered, "Do you think this could be...?"

I shuddered. "It's possible. The police need to get fingerprints and have this analyzed."

Jake's eyebrows shot up as he turned back to us. "I've called the police. They are on the way. In the meantime, don't touch—" His voice cut off as he spotted the dagger in my hands.

His face paled, making his chiseled features even more striking. "Where did you find that?"

I explained hastily while Jake examined the weapon, his jaw set firmly. "This looks disturbingly similar to daggers that went missing from our collection years ago. I fear the killer wanted to retrieve this to cover their tracks."

Voices echoed from the hallway. The police had already arrived. Jake leaned in closer, his voice barely above a whisper. "Hide that dagger and don't mention it for now. I don't fully trust the police or the museum—there are too many secrets here that certain people want to stay buried."

"But Jake, it has dried blood on it. It could be the murder weapon."

"Lola, I know this sounds strange and like I am guilty of something, but this is important. I need you to keep this safe. It could prove my innocence one day. Meet me tonight, and I'll tell you everything I know."

Before I could respond, Detective Harry Lewis entered with a team of forensics experts. I hesitated. Harry and I were good friends with possibilities of more. I felt so guilty about not giving the dagger to Harry, but I also sensed there was a lot more I needed to figure out. I slid the dagger into my bag, pulse racing, as I wondered just how deep this mystery would go.

Jake caught my eye briefly, a warning in his stare, telling me to keep silent for now. He hesitated, then added, "There's something I should share with you about my family and the Worthingtons ... it could shed light on our current predicament. But not here, not now. Tonight, I promise. You said you owned at the Gallery Café, right?"

Polly and I walked side by side, the day's events weighing heavily on our minds. The afternoon passed in a blur as we busied ourselves at the Café, training our new employee, Thomas, and serving our regulars. Amidst the hustle and bustle, I felt a thrum of anticipation for our rendezvous with Jake.

Before he arrived, I hid the dagger and the key in a secret compartment under the floorboards of the café. I didn't want to risk carrying them around, especially if Jake's suspicions about the police were true.

What had Jake meant about his family and the Worthingtons? His casual charm made it difficult to determine his motives. I felt torn between trusting his offer of help and fearing what secrets the night might reveal.

As evening fell and the café closed for the night, Polly and I settled into our favorite booth with iced teas in hand. "Crazy day, right?" Polly remarked.

Before I could reply, she added, teasing, "So, you and Jake, huh? He's quite the dashing mystery man. Admit it, Lola, you're a bit smitten. But don't worry, I won't tell Harry that he has competition in the crush department."

I scoffed, but my cheeks burned, betraying me. "He's helping us, Polly. That's all. Besides, we don't even know if we can trust him yet."

She grinned, wiggling her eyebrows. "Whatever you say, Lola. Just don't forget we're in this together, and not all handsome strangers have our best interests at heart."

The little bell above the door jingled. Jake sauntered in, looking effortlessly dashing in a worn leather jacket that hugged his broad shoulders. His dark hair had been tousled by the wind, and his blue eyes sparkled with mischief. "Mind if I crash the party? I brought my own mask, just in case you didn't want anyone to know I was here."

As Jake made the quip about the mask, I found myself briefly wondering what Harry would think if he saw him there.

He grew serious, pulling up a chair. "We need to chat about the museum. There are things going on you should know about."

Polly and I leaned in, intrigued. Jake continued, "The Worthingt ons... They'll do anything to keep control. And my family, well, we've had our fair share of conflicts with them."

Just then, Tetley let out a sharp cry from behind the counter. I turned to see him perched by the kitchen window, nose twitching urgently. "What's up, little guy?"

Tetley pawed at the window, fixated on the alley outside. An uneasy feeling hit that we weren't alone. I checked the window but saw only shadows.

"Stay here," Jake said quietly, his eyes scanning the dark alley. "I'll go check it out."

I looked through the window but saw only shadows. A chill ran down my spine, reminding me of the dagger's cold metal when I placed it under the floorboards.

Chapter 3

The alley looked empty, yet unease still churned in my stomach. Jake returned, brow furrowed. "Must have just been a stray cat. But we should be careful."

Polly leaned forward, eyes gleaming. "So, what were you saying about the Worthingtons and the museum board?"

Jake sighed, running a hand through his hair. "The board members all stand to gain control and money with Worthington gone. They've been trying to push him out for years. And my family ... we once owned part of this museum. There were disputes over artifacts, and Worthington claimed full ownership. But I think some items were obtained illegally."

Polly chimed in, "Wow, sounds like a proper soap opera. Artifacts, power struggles, and hostile takeovers—all that's missing is an evil twin."

Jake let out a little chortle, but his jaw tensed as he spoke of Worthington. "He engineered some hostile takeover of the museum to seize power from the board of directors and my grandfather's estate. Claimed we were mismanaging funds and not acquiring notable enough exhibits. He went to great lengths to satisfy his own vanity in building 'the most prestigious private museum in the country' with no respect for how it once was."

"This sounds dangerous," I said. "But it gives several motives for murder. We should look into the board members."

Jake nodded. "I can get you access to the museum records and security footage. See if anything seems amiss."

"And we can question the board members at the next fundraising gala!" Polly added eagerly.

I laughed at her enthusiasm, though worry lingered. Were we in over our heads? Still, solving this mystery felt thrilling—especially with Jake as a partner in crime.

The next day at the café, Detective Harry stopped by for his usual coffee and croissant. His eyes fell on Jake, and a flicker of annoyance crossed his face.

"Who's that?" Harry asked, a slight edge to his friendly tone.

"Just a ... friend," I said. "Just came in for some coffee and conversation."

Harry raised an eyebrow but said nothing more. We had been flirting for months, though he was usually all work and little play. But his jaw seemed more tense today, his gazes lingering on me when he thought I wasn't looking. Was he ... jealous? The idea sent a little thrill through me, even as guilt hit. I valued Harry's friendship, yet whatever was blossoming with Jake felt new and intoxicating.

After Harry left, I turned to find Jake studying me, a teasing look in his eyes. "I think the good detective sees me as competition. He's quite smitten with you." Jake chuckled, "I'm surprised he didn't ask for my full background check on the spot. It's good to keep friends close, and potential rivals even closer."

I blushed. "Don't be ridiculous. Harry and I are just friends." Even as I said it, I wondered if I was trying to convince myself.

Jake grinned, leaning in close. "If you say so. But I also think you feel ... this energy ... between you and me."

My breath caught as I stared into his blue eyes. He was infatuating. I couldn't deny the connection—or the longing building inside me to kiss those teasing lips.

Jake slid into the booth, dropping a thick file folder onto the table. "I've found our first lead. Brittany DuPont, notorious art collector and Worthington's biggest rival."

Polly smirked, "Brittany DuPont? With a name like that, she's either a master art collector or a pop star's alter ego."

"How did you get all this information on Brittany?" I asked curiously.

Jake grinned. "As a museum guard, I have access to records the public doesn't see. Background checks on important donors and collectors are standard. And she has an office in the museum ... and ... she is my aunt."

Polly and I both looked at each other, a little surprised, but Jake told us 'his family' and the Worthingtons had been at odds for years.

After a few moments' hesitation, Polly leaned forward eagerly. "What did you find out?"

"Brittany has been trying to outbid Worthington for years but could never match his deep pockets. Sources say she was furious. He snatched up three rare paintings she desperately wanted. Her resentment could have built into murderous rage. And with her connections, she could pull something like this off."

"She does sound suspicious," I agreed. "But we should hear her side before accusing her of murder."

Polly's eyes gleamed with excitement. "I know—we should pay her an unexpected visit at her estate. Catch her off guard so she'll spill the beans!"

I laughed at her enthusiasm. "Slow down, detective. A formal interview might be better."

Jake grinned, eyes twinkling. "I have a better idea. Brittany's estate has exquisite gardens she opens for charity events. We could visit during open hours and run into her there, where she may be more inclined to chat freely."

Polly grinned, "Going undercover as garden enthusiasts? I love it! I'll practice my best 'oohs' and 'aahs' for the flowers."

The next day, we set off for Brittany's estate on the outskirts of Fawnwood. Verdant gardens bursting with colorful blossoms surrounded an imposing Georgian manor house. Brittany stood by the rose garden, instructing gardeners with a stern sweep of her arm.

She turned as we approached, eyeing us suspiciously. "May I help you?"

"We're visiting from the Gallery Café and wanted to compliment your lovely gardens," I offered smoothly.

Brittany sniffed. "How quaint. Well, enjoy." She turned away, dismissing us.

Polly frowned. This icy reception would make gleaning information difficult. I racked my brain for a way to thaw Brittany's frosty demeanor, hoping the visit hadn't been in vain.

I attempted some small talk. "You know, your roses are almost as captivating as your art collection. It's hard to choose a favorite." Brittany paused, turning back to face us with a slightly raised eyebrow. She was a tall, elegant woman in her late forties, with jet black hair pulled back into a bun so tight it could pass as a facelift, and piercing green eyes that seemed to see right through you.

"Indeed? Well, they say that beauty is in the eye of the beholder," she replied, her tone warmer than before. We had her attention, for now.

Polly jumped in, feigning amazement at a nearby flower. "Oh, my goodness, is this a 'Blue Moon' rose? I've never seen one in person before! It's absolutely stunning."

Brittany's eyes flickered with interest. "You have a keen eye. It's one of my prized blooms. I had to search far and wide to find it—I'm pretty sure I've accumulated enough frequent flyer miles to circle the globe a few times. They say it's as rare as the paintings in my collection."

Polly, seizing the opportunity, smoothly interjected, "Speaking of paintings, we heard about the recent competition between you and Worthington. It must have been quite a rivalry."

A shadow crossed Brittany's face as she hesitated, then sighed. "Yes, it was ... intense. But that's the art world for you. Everyone wants to be on top, and Worthington was no exception."

I probed further, "Were you at the masquerade ball when Worthington was killed?

Brittany narrowed her eyes, seemingly evaluating our intentions. After a moment, she said, "I was there, but I left early, before the murder occurred. I have witnesses to confirm where I was. And as for the rivalry, I can't deny that I resented Worthington for acquiring the paintings I had my eye on. Are you suggesting that I'd resort to murder? That's preposterous."

Polly, ever the bold one, pressed on. "But you do admit you had a motive, and with your connections, you could have arranged for his death."

Brittany scoffed, "If I wanted Worthington's collection, I would have acquired it the same way I've always done—by outbidding and outsmarting my opponents. I'm not some common criminal."

As we continued to question Brittany, Polly subtly snapped a few pictures of the garden with her phone, capturing the surroundings. The garden itself seemed to hold secrets, with its winding paths, hidden nooks, and rare plants. It was a place where anything could be concealed or discovered.

As our conversation drew to a close, Brittany looked at us with a mix of amusement and suspicion. "I hope I've satisfied your curiosity. Now, if you'll excuse me, I have a garden to tend to."

As we left her estate, Polly shared the photos she'd taken. One image stood out: a small, inconspicuous door hidden behind a thicket of bushes. It seemed out of place in the otherwise meticulously planned garden.

"Interesting," I mused, studying the photo. "What do you think that door leads to?"

Polly's eyes widened. "Maybe it's a secret passage, or a hidden room where Brittany keeps her most valuable treasures. Perhaps even something she doesn't want anyone to know about. Or perhaps it's just a cleverly disguised tool shed."

Chapter 4

The jarring crash of shattering china cut through our discussion like a knife. I whipped around to find Thomas, my eager yet bumbling new barista, kneeling amidst a sea of broken crockery and glistening shards.

"So sorry, my fault, so clumsy, won't happen again!" Thomas sputtered, hands fluttering about uselessly as he attempted to gather up the remnants of what was once a full tea set.

Polly snorted into her coffee, shaking with silent giggles at the absurd spectacle. I bit my lip to keep from laughing at Thomas's panic-stricken expression and anxious flapping movements, which only resulted in slicing his fingers on the razor-sharp edges.

"Calm down before you hurt yourself again, and go get a dustpan," I said. Thomas nodded vigorously, nearly slipping on the debris underfoot in his haste to obey.

Polly snorted again. "Well, you certainly weren't exaggerating about the entertainment factor of our new staff!"

"I should start selling tickets," I replied wryly. "The comedy stylings of Thomas the Barista—he'll have you in stitches, whether he means to or not."

Another crash echoed from the kitchen, followed by a muffled "Sorry!" from Thomas. Polly and I looked at each other and dissolved into laughter.

When I could breathe again, I wiped my eyes and sighed. "At least the job is never dull. But we should probably supervise Thomas before he destroys the place. The china massacre is enough excitement for one day."

Polly grinned. "Too right. Amateur sleuthing is tame compared to the daily drama around here!"

Polly and I made our way to the kitchen, bracing ourselves for whatever chaos Thomas had unleashed. But as we pushed open the swinging doors, the scent of cinnamon and roasted coffee beans wafted out—Thomas seemed to have found his rhythm again.

He looked up from brewing a fresh pot of coffee, flashing us a sheepish grin. "Sorry again for the mess. I'll be more careful, I swear!"

I smiled, relief flooding me. "Just take it slow. No need to rush." Thomas nodded, turning back to his work with a look of renewed determination. "And, thanks for making the coffee, but don't forget to go out front and clean up the first mess."

Thomas hit the heel of his hand on his forehead. "Oh, yeah, right. I forgot about the old mess when I created the new mess. Sorry." Thomas quickly grabbed the broom and dustpan and headed out front.

As Polly and I returned to our table, my phone buzzed with an incoming message. "It's from Jake." My pulse quickened, reading his name. "He says the museum's head curator, Victor, is acting strange. Worth keeping an eye on."

Polly leaned forward eagerly. "The curator? But he's been there for years. Why is Jake suspicious of him now?"

I scanned Jake's message again, lingering over his playful sign-off. "Apparently, Victor disagreed with Worthington's vision for new exhibits. And now, with Worthington gone, Victor has control again."

"Motive and means," Polly mused.

"We should talk to Victor. See if we can find any cracks." I typed a quick reply to Jake, hoping to see him at the museum.

The museum towered before us, pristine white marble gleaming in the afternoon sun. Polly and I exchanged a glance before pushing open the grand doors.

Jake waved us over, a frown creasing his forehead. My breath caught at his roguish smile. "Victor's been acting twitchy all morning. Keeps disappearing into the archives. I think I should tell you, Victor is my cousin, Victor DuPont. Really something like first cousin once removed or something odd like that. My grandfather, Elias, and his father Ezekiel are brothers. Almost no one knows that. He always acts like he doesn't know me."

Polly and I both looked at him a bit puzzled but said nothing. I tucked this information away to dwell on more later.

"The archives could hide many secrets," Polly broke the brief silence. Jake led us through opulent galleries, but tension thrummed through the calm.

Rounding a corner, we nearly collided with Victor barking orders at museum attendants hauling a massive marble statue. "Careful, you oafs! That's a priceless antiquity!"

Victor's eyes narrowed as he spotted us. "What are you doing here? The museum is preparing a new exhibit."

"We wanted to speak with you about Worthington," I said smoothly.

A flicker of annoyance crossed Victor's face before he plastered on a smile. "Tragic loss. But we must continue his vision." Victor strode off down the hall after the attendants, coattails flapping.

We hurried after him, but a set of heavy oak doors slammed in our faces. Polly jiggled the handles to no avail. "Locked! How rude."

Jake examined the lock, frowning. "This will take time to pick. But there may be another way in." His eyes twinkled mischievously.

We followed Jake down a dim passage. Cobwebs clung to corners, and a musty scent filled the air.

Jake gestured to a narrow grate. "Air ducts connect throughout. We can crawl through to spy on Victor!"

Polly grimaced. "What if we get stuck?"

Jake grinned. "Where's your sense of adventure?"

Jake pried open the grate and peered into the darkness. "Coast is clear. But we'll have to move quietly—sound carries in these old vents."

Polly looked at me dubiously. "If I get stuck, I'm blaming you two."

Jake's eyes gleamed. "Where's the fun without a little risk? Now, ladies first..."

I hoisted myself up into the narrow vent, cobwebs brushing against my face. The metal groaned under our weight as Jake and Polly followed. We crawled in silence, following the distant sounds of Victor berating his staff.

After a few turns, faint light filtered through slats in another grate ahead. I peered through to see Victor meticulously examining a newly arrived artifact. Something about his keen, almost reverent interest sent a shiver down my spine.

I lay down so Polly could see over me, but it wasn't Polly behind me as I thought.

Jake leaned close to get a better view, his breath warm on my cheek. I swallowed hard, heartbeat quickening. Focus, I reminded myself, tearing my gaze from those mischievous blue eyes.

Then Jake leaned left so that Polly could at least see a little from the right. I really don't know how we all fit into that space.

Victor held the artifact up to the light, a satisfied smile crossing his face. "At last, a piece worthy of my collection. The board will have to see that my way is best... if I tell them about this one."

Polly's eyes went wide. "Is that...?" She slapped a hand over her mouth too late. The vent groaned loudly under us.

Victor's head snapped up. We froze in place, not even daring to breathe. After an endless moment, Victor finally shrugged and turned away, locking the artifact in a cabinet.

We scrambled out of the vent, dusting ourselves off as my mind raced over what we had just witnessed. Victor was hiding valuable artifacts in his museum, but why?

Polly paced the floor, brow furrowed in thought. "The way Victor examined that artifact ... he seemed almost reverent. But why lock it away and not display it properly?"

"You're right, it doesn't add up." I leaned against the wall, arms folded. "Victor's role as curator is to collect and showcase important relics. Hiding them contradicts that. Unless..."

"He doesn't actually want anyone to see them." Jake finished my thought, eyes gleaming with curiosity. "Seems our curator may be amassing secret treasures for himself."

I gasped. "He wouldn't dare steal from his own museum!"

Jake shrugged. "Desperate men do desperate things. And Victor was clearly annoyed by Worthington's meddling..."

"You think Worthington discovered Victor's scheme, so Victor ... disposed of him?" Polly looked stunned by the implication.

My heart raced as the pieces began falling into place. "It all fits. The artifacts, Victor's strange behavior, Worthington's untimely end. We have to find a way to expose Victor's crimes!"

Jake squeezed my hand, eyes burning into mine. "Whatever it takes. I won't let him get away with betraying the public's trust like this." I swallowed hard at the fierceness in his voice, the threat looming over us.

Chapter 5

The Gallery Café was a battlefield of culinary mishaps as I received news of fresh disasters from my well-meaning, yet catastrophically clumsy barista, Thomas. A broken espresso machine, scalded milk flooding the counter, and a tray of pastries tumbling onto the floor—all within the span of an hour. I rubbed my temples, feeling the beginnings of a headache coming on.

Polly stifled a laugh upon seeing my expression. "Really outdid himself today, didn't he?"

I sighed. "At this rate, the insurance premiums will bankrupt me. But at least the entertainment is free..."

A familiar voice spoke behind me. "Rough day?" I turned to find Jake leaning against the café counter, a roguish grin lighting up his face. My breath caught as our eyes met.

Behind the counter, Thomas emerged from the kitchen—strangely out of his usual café uniform jacket. Instead, he wore a button-down shirt and apron as he carried a tray of fresh pastries to the display. Had he spilled something on himself too? I made a mental note to check in on him, hoping today's disasters were at an end.

Polly glanced between us knowingly. "I'll just ... go check on Thomas. Make sure something else isn't on fire." She slipped into the kitchen, the door swinging shut behind her.

An awkward silence lingered as Jake and I were left alone. My heart raced being so close to him, but I forced myself to remain professional. There were bigger mysteries afoot than my silly crush.

Jake's playful manner faded as he spoke. "We need to find solid proof of Victor's crimes. Before the trail goes cold."

I nodded. "You're right. His suspicious behavior and that hidden artifact are a start ... but we'll need more. His office and records may hold the key."

"Then tonight, let's search for clues. Meet me after closing, and we'll try to find more information that may help us." Jake's eyes gleamed with determination.

He turned to leave, but I grabbed his arm to get his attention. "Jake, I ... just be careful. Victor seems dangerous. Don't do anything reckless." I hoped my concern didn't betray my feelings, but his safety mattered more.

Jake gave me a solemn nod. "You be careful too. We'll crack this case, don't worry." He flashed a quick grin before disappearing out the door.

I stared after him, heart swelling. Sentiment would have to wait—we had a mystery to unravel, and a long night ahead. The truth was out there ... we just had to survive finding it.

I heard another crash in the kitchen and sighed. At least the café had survived Thomas for one more day ... if only just barely.

After the chaos of the day, closing the Gallery Café for the evening came as a relief. Polly and I wiped down tables as the aroma of coffee still lingered. We counted the till, eager to head home as my feet ached from rushing around all day.

Polly chuckled, dropping coins into the register. "At this rate, Thomas will have the place condemned by month's end!"

I smiled wearily, massaging my temples. "Let's just be grateful we survived another day." The café had only just been rebuilt, and Thomas seemed bent on destroying it once more.

The cool evening breeze carried the scent of fall leaves and chimney smoke. We locked up and strolled down cobblestone streets aglow under amber streetlamps. The familiar aroma of garlic and breadsticks wafted from our neighborhood Italian restaurant, Giovanni's Bistro, a comforting haven.

"Lola, Polly! The usual?" Tony called, leaning against the counter drying his hands on an apron, the sleeves of his pale blue button-down, rolled up to the elbows.

We nodded, settling into red vinyl chairs as Tony busied himself with two plates of rosemary chicken and pasta primavera.

Polly glanced at me over her water glass, eyes gleaming with mischief. "So, you and Jake seemed rather cozy today. Care to share?"

I felt heat rise in my cheeks. "We're just friends," I insisted, though the quiver in my voice betrayed me. Harry and I had a complicated history, but he seemed to be thawing. I knew beneath his serious demeanor beat a kind heart.

The bell above the door jingled, and in walked Harry. My heart skipped a beat, an involuntary reaction that I'd come to associate with his presence. He strode in, his chestnut hair tousled as if he had just run his fingers through it, and his warm brown eyes immediately found mine.

Harry's smile faded. Though he had ended things with his girl-friend, my closeness with Jake now loomed between us. An uneasy silence fell, tension filling the space where sentiment once lived.

Harry cleared his throat. "Evening, ladies. Out for the evening, I see." His eyes drifted back to me, eyes clouded with memories of what might have been.

I exhaled, shoulders tight. "An evening of rest, hopefully. If Fawn-wood's villains allow it." Our encounters were bittersweet, a reminder of roads not taken.

Harry nodded, a frown creasing his brow. "Let's hope so." As a policeman, worry came as second nature—and though our bond had shifted, his protectiveness remained. His eyes lingered, words left un-spoken, before he turned away. "Take care, ladies."

Harry paid for his carryout order and left. When the door swung shut behind him, I released a breath, heart swelling with wistfulness at the love that barely smoldered and the danger I could not escape. Harry understood, though knowing brought scant comfort.

Polly's teasing grin had faded. "Quite the tangle, with him investi-gating the same villains that we are looking into, huh?"

I smiled grimly. "The only mystery I care to solve is how Tony always manages to have just enough garlic bread left for us, even at closing time. It's like he has a sixth sense for our carb cravings."

Tony arrived at our table, bearing two steaming plates of our fa-vorites—rosemary chicken and pasta primavera. His warm smile was a welcome ending to an otherwise chaotic day. The scent of garlic and fresh basil wafted up, wrapping us in the comforting familiarity of the neighborhood bistro. As we dug into our meals, the trials of the day seemed to melt away with each delicious bite. However, my meeting at the museum was looming on the horizon. Despite the comforting aroma of garlic and basil, a hint of anxiety bubbled up at the thought of the coming search for clues. I felt a pang of worry for Jake. His fearless determination to uncover the truth often led him towards danger. As I twirled the pasta around my fork, I found my thoughts drifting back to him. The mystery of Victor's hidden artifact, Jake's brave resolve, and the tangled emotions I felt for both him and Harry, it was enough to lose my appetite. But for now, I pushed those thoughts aside, savoring these last peaceful moments.

After bidding Tony goodnight, Polly and I walked along the cobblestone streets once more. The night was cool, and a sense of unease prickled at the back of my neck as we made our way to the museum.

Just then, a flutter of movement caught my attention. Above us, a curtain danced in the breeze from an open window of a grand townhouse. A woman's silhouette paced within, her figure framed by the glow of indoor lighting. I recognized her instantly. It was Marcella DuPont, Brittany's socialite cousin.

Marcella's lifestyle was one of luxury and philanthropy, both of which were largely underwritten by Worthington's wealth. I remembered a charity gala I had attended last year, held at the Worthington estate. Marcella had been a radiant hostess, working the crowd with her charm and vivacity. Her silk gown shimmered, her diamond necklace sparkled, and the entire spectacle was funded by Worthington's deep pockets. Even her own estate and her charitable endeavors were known to be backed by him. His sudden death, I realized, might destabilize her comfortable existence.

As she noticed us, a fleeting look of alarm crossed Marcella's face before she retreated from the window, letting the curtain fall back into place.

"Did you see...?" I began, my heart pounding in my chest.

Polly's response was a grave nod. "Marcella DuPont," she said. "This just got more complicated. If Worthington's death affects her lifestyle, she could now have a lot more to lose. "

Chapter 6

The museum, usually a place of grandeur and solemnity, had transformed into an enchanting labyrinth under the spell of night. It seemed to radiate a peculiar coziness, its honey-colored stone warmed by the soft glow of the carefully placed spotlights. Jake had let us in through the side entrance reserved for staff and special guests, a secret door veiled by an old ivy-covered wall.

Jake first led us to the furnace room. "I need to check on the heat really quickly."

Working late into the night, Jake had an odd yet endearing obsession with the museum's elderly heating system. It was an eccentric antique, just like many of the pieces in the museum, and it required a kind of a tender care that only Jake seemed to understand. "The old girl gets temperamental when the nights get chilly," Jake explained, patting the ancient furnace affectionately.

The reason we were meeting him here, though, was far more serious. The museum was under threat, a fact that had surfaced under dire circumstances. We made our way to Victor's office. The documents strewn haphazardly across Victor's mahogany desk bore testament to those dire circumstances.

Jake picked up a sheaf of papers, his face stern. "Worthington had been negotiating to sell the museum land," he revealed, his voice echoing slightly in the high-ceilinged room. "He had the audacity to plan this while Victor was making plans for acquisitions and expansions."

I gasped. "That's ... that's unthinkable! The museum is a historic site, a part of Fawnwood's soul."

Polly's lips thinned. "And it makes Victor a prime suspect. He's always been fiercely protective of the museum. This ... betrayal could have sparked a deadly outrage."

Jake nodded, his face intense. "Victor was livid. There are accounts of a heated argument between him and Worthington. But there's more..."

Jake rifled through the papers, frown deepening. "There are letters here detailing Worthington's schemes to fund speculative investments ... by selling prime real estate, including the museum land."

I felt faint. "Selling a historic site? That's monstrous!" The museum stood as a monument to Fawnwood's past, housing treasures that could never be replaced. Its destruction was unthinkable.

Polly's eyes gleamed with anger. "Worthington's greed knew no bounds. But this gives Victor clear motive for revenge." She turned to Jake. "The argument between them - how heated did it become?"

Jake sighed. "According to witness accounts, Victor threatened to resign in protest. Worthington taunted him, saying he could easily replace a museum director. Victor was livid."

I shuddered, imagining the fury Victor must have felt. A life's work and passion, callously disregarded and under threat of annihilation. "Betrayal can be a potent motive for violence. And Victor has always been fiercely devoted to the museum."

"Devoted to exclusion of all else," Jake added grimly. He held up a small key. "This opens a locked drawer in Victor's desk. I found documents detailing the argument ... and plans for confronting Worthington again."

My heart pounded as Jake slid the key into the lock, turning it with a dull click. He pulled open the drawer, searching its contents. His expression shifted, eyes widening.

"What is it?" I asked, pulse racing.

Jake looked up slowly, color draining from his face. "Plane tickets for a swift departure ... dated the day after Worthington's murder."

As the shock of Jake's discovery lingered in the air, our attention was abruptly drawn to the sound of footsteps echoing in the cavernous gallery outside Victor's office. The museum, usually a tranquil haven, felt different at night, its every creak and whisper amplified in the stillness. We exchanged a glance, knowing that we should be the only ones in the museum at this hour.

"Hide," Jake whispered, quickly sweeping the incriminating documents back into the drawer. He flicked off the desk lamp, plunging the room into darkness. The only light came from the moon, its silvery glow filtering through the tall, narrow windows.

We scrambled behind a large display case filled with ancient Roman glassware, the vibrant colors barely visible in the dim light. My heart pounded in my chest as the footsteps grew louder. I peeked around the corner of the case, my eyes straining to see who was coming.

The door creaked open, and in walked Marcella DuPont, her silhouette framed by the faint light in the hallway. She was clad in an extravagant fur coat, looking wildly out of place in the museum's austere setting.

"What on earth...?" I muttered, more to myself than to Jake or Polly. Marcella had no business here, especially at this late hour.

She moved to the desk, flipping on the desk lamp and revealing a distressed look on her face. She began rifling through the papers on the desk, her furrowed brow showing she was looking for something.

Jake was about to move, but Polly held him back. "Wait," she whispered. "Let's see what she's up to."

Marcella pulled out a drawer, frustration clear on her face when she didn't find what she was looking for. She closed it and opened another, her actions growing more frantic.

Finally, she stood up, pushing the chair back so abruptly that it crashed onto the floor. She looked around the room, her eyes filled with a mixture of fear and desperation. Then, taking a deep breath, she turned and walked out of the room, leaving the door ajar.

We waited until her footsteps had receded before coming out of our hiding place. Jake turned the lamp back on, illuminating the chaos Marcella had left in her wake.

"Marcella DuPont," Polly muttered. "What is she doing snooping around Victor's office?"

"Whatever it is, it's not good," I said, my mind whirring with possibilities. "We need to find out what she was looking for. And why she's involved in this at all?"

Jake nodded, his face grim. "This just got a lot more complicated."

Chapter 7

Morning light streamed through the windows, casting a warm glow on the cozy kitchen of our apartment. It was a refreshing change of scene, a contrast to the eerie silence of the museum at night. The aroma of brewing coffee mingled with the sweet scent of pancakes, creating a comforting symphony of breakfast smells. I watched as Polly, with a practiced ease, flipped a golden-brown pancake into the air. It spun gracefully before landing back into the pan, an acrobat completing a perfect somersault. Our kitchen, bathed in the soft morning light, hummed with the gentle rhythm of our long-standing friendship.

"Remember the time in high school when we tried to solve the mystery of who stole Principal Brown's trophy?" Polly asked, a mischievous glint in her eyes. She slid a golden-brown pancake onto my plate.

I laughed. "How could I forget? We turned the whole school upside down!" We had always shared a passion for puzzles and mysteries, a bond that had only grown stronger over the years.

"You look bright-eyed for so early," I teased as she sat down. "What have you discovered that's got you so animated?"

"I did some digging into Marcella's background," Polly said. "Earlier this year, she was briefly a person of interest in an arson case. A historic barn was burned, and anonymous tips led the police to question her, though she was never officially charged."

My eyes widened. Troubling as this news was, Marcella's suspicious past might explain her odd behavior and if she relied on Worthington's money, it could provide a motive for breaking into Victor's office. "That's quite a discovery," I replied. "But after what we witnessed last night, perhaps not entirely surprising."

Polly nodded. "She had an ironclad alibi, and the police — allegedly — received false tips intended to frame her. She appears to have been the target of malicious lies, not an arsonist."

I sighed, stirring my coffee as I processed this new information. If Marcella was innocent in that old case, why was she sneaking around the museum after dark? The mystery surrounding her refused to unravel easily.

A buzz from Polly's phone interrupted my thoughts. "It's an alert I set up," she explained, tapping the screen. Her eyes widened as she read the news bulletin.

"What is it?" I asked, pulse quickening.

Polly looked up, an odd mix of excitement and apprehension in her eyes. "They're demolishing the old fire-damaged barn on the DuPont estate ... today. According to this alert, the crews just arrived to start working."

A chill crept down my spine. I've known Marcella a long time, though not close by any means. I think it is totally possible that abandoned barn held secrets from Marcella's past, ones she had gone to great lengths to bury. Its ruins likely contained clues worth searching for—and destroying.

The rumble of heavy machinery echoed in the distance as Polly and I approached the DuPont estate through the woods. We thought it best to park the car outside the grounds and enter on foot. The sprawling property was a rich tapestry of gardens, meadows, and clusters of old oaks, with the stately manor house rising from its heart like a grand dame. But it was the dilapidated barn, set on the farthest corner of the estate, that had drawn us here.

"There's a weird smell of decay in the air — or is that just my imagination?" I pondered.

Polly shivered. "There's definitely something that smells off around here — but we'll get to the bottom of it."

The air was thick with dust and the smell of freshly churned soil. Men in hard hats bustled about, their fluorescent vests creating a stark contrast against the morning haze. A bulldozer idled nearby, its jaws poised ominously over the charred remnants of the barn.

"Hold on," a voice boomed as we approached the cordoned off area. A man with a grizzled beard and weathered face approached us, a hard hat clutched in his beefy hand. "This area is off-limits."

Polly stepped forward, her voice steady. "We're here on behalf of the Fawnwood Historical Society," she said, flashing an old library card that bore the society's logo. "We believe this barn may have historical significance."

The man squinted at the card, then at us. After a moment's hesitation, he nodded. "Alright, but be quick. And mind the loose floorboards."

Heart pounding, I followed Polly into the skeletal remains of the barn. The inside of the barn felt like a forgotten memory, filled with the scent of old wood and the acrid tang of smoke. The fire had left its savage signature everywhere - blackened beams reached out like skeletal arms and charred floorboards groaned under our weight. Each step we took seemed to stir the ghosts of the past, unsettling a disquiet that hung in the air.

"We're looking for anything that might connect Marcella to the arson," Polly whispered, her flashlight beam cutting through the gloom. "Clues, evidence, anything."

The barn groaned around us, a soft lament echoing through the ruins. I bit my lip, my eyes sweeping over the shadows. "You think she might have left something behind?"

Polly shrugged, her attention focused on the pile of debris near the back. "Arsonists sometimes return to the scene of the crime. It's a compulsion, almost."

I nodded, the chilling thought sending a shiver down my spine. We split up, each taking a side of the barn. Time felt warped inside the barn, the outside world muffled by the thick wooden walls. I was so engrossed in my search that I almost missed it.

"Polly," I called, crouching to inspect the item. It was a small, metallic object, half buried in the ash and debris. With a rush of excitement, I called out again. "Polly, I think I've found something!"

Using a stick, I carefully extricated it. As I brushed off the ash, I just let out a disappointed sigh.

In my hand, glinting in the light of my flashlight, was just an old coin.

Polly ran over to where I stood. "Never mind, it's just an old coin, although it is unusual."

"Let me see. It could be something, it looks ancient." Polly said. I slipped it into my pocket and continued to search.

Suddenly, the rumble of the bulldozer drew closer. Our eyes widened in alarm. The operator, a burly man with a hard hat and reflective vest, was back in his seat, preparing to resume his work.

"Hey, you two!" he shouted, spotting us. "You need to clear out now!"

Polly and I glanced at each other, panic welling up. We couldn't just leave; we had barely scratched the surface of our investigation. But we couldn't afford to draw attention or arouse suspicion either. We had found no leads, but we knew something had to be in here.

Thinking fast, Polly waved at the man. "Just a moment!" she called back. "We think we've found a colony of endangered bats!"

The man paused, frowning. "Bats?"

"Yes! And if this barn is their habitat, you might need to halt the demolition!" Polly shouted, feigning concern.

The man grumbled something under his breath and clambered down from his machine, lumbering over. Meanwhile, I seized the opportunity to quickly scan the area one more time. To my left, something caught my eye: another old coin, nearly buried under a pile of charred wood. I grabbed it, hiding it in my pocket just as the man reached us.

"Where are these bats, then?" he asked, skeptically peering around.

Feigning disappointment, Polly pointed vaguely at the rafters. "They seem to have flown off. Perhaps the noise scared them. But you should definitely have a specialist check it out."

The man grumbled again but agreed to call a pest control company to examine the barn before proceeding. As he walked off, Polly and I let out a collective sigh of relief.

"Good thinking with the bats," I said, grinning at her.

Polly just chuckled, her eyes sparkling with adrenaline. "Now, let's keep searching while we can. I found a second coin just as that guy came in. Look."

"Could those coins belong to Marcella?" Polly mused, turning the coin over in her hands. "They look like unusual pieces as coins go, not the ordinary quarter..."

I shrugged, unable to answer.

"We should get it to an expert," Polly said. "See if they can identify the coin, where it came from, the age, that sort of thing.

Her words trailed off as a strange sound echoed through the barn. It was a low growl, reverberating off the old wooden walls. Our eyes met, reflecting mutual confusion and a hint of alarm.

The ground beneath us shuddered, and we both instinctively reached out to steady each other. Dust rained from the rafters, peppering our hair and shoulders. The barn groaned in protest as the vibrations grew stronger.

"What's happening?" I asked, my voice barely above a whisper.

Polly squinted through the dust-choked air towards the entrance. "That's... not the bulldozer."

And then we saw it - a sleek black vehicle tearing across the open field towards the barn. Its engine roared like a wild beast, the sound growing louder as it neared. The driver was a silhouette behind the glare of the windshield, but the intent was clear.

"They're not slowing down," Polly said, her voice tight. She grabbed my arm, her grip like iron. "We need to move. Now!"

Chapter 8

"Polly, run!" I screamed, yanking her arm towards the back of the barn.

The SUV careened into the barn, missing us by inches as we threw ourselves out of its path. We scrambled behind a stack of crates as the vehicle slammed on brakes and slid to a stop; the commotion shaking the foundations of the old building. The smell of gasoline, dust, and old wood filled my nostrils as my ears rang from the deafening sound of the horn.

The barn groaned, its old foundation shuddering under the violent invasion.

"Climb!" Polly yelled, pointing towards a series of wooden beams that led upwards. With adrenaline fueling our every move, we scrambled up, each grab, each foothold, a desperate bid for survival.

We reached a small loft just as the barn gave an especially violent shudder. Below us, the dust was settling, revealing the vehicle—a large black SUV—wedged halfway into the barn. Suddenly, a piercing beam of light shot upwards, just narrowly missing our hiding spot.

Its engine still hummed menacingly, and the tinted windows concealed the driver's identity.

"Could it be Marcella?" I whispered, eyeing the SUV.

Polly shook her head, her face pale but determined. "I can't tell from here. But whoever it is either wants something or wants to keep others from finding something."

The SUV's headlights flickered on, piercing the dust-choked air of the barn. They began scanning the debris, the movements methodical and purposeful. It clicked in my mind then—they were looking for what, the coin, something we had missed, what?

"We can't let them find us," I muttered, glancing at Polly. She nodded, her face set in a grim line.

"We need a distraction," she said, her eyes scanning the loft. Her eyes landed on a pile of old farming equipment, rusted and forgotten. A large, hefty looking pitchfork lay atop the pile.

Without uttering a word, Polly silently made her way to the pitchfork. She hefted it, testing its weight, then shot me a look filled with resolve. With a swift movement, she hurled it towards the far corner of the barn. It landed with a loud clatter, echoing through the barn and causing the beam of light to jerk towards the sound. When it did, we could see the person holding the spotlight was indeed Marcella DuPont.

Seizing the opportunity, we slid down the wooden beams, hitting the ground running. Behind us, we could hear the SUV's engine revving, but we didn't dare look back. We sprinted across the open field for the woods as fast as our legs would take us.

Finally, panting and out of breath, we reached the edge of the woods. Leaning against a tree, we caught our breath. The distant rumble of an engine revving up jolted us from our brief respite, and we headed deeper into the woods towards the car.

"That was too close," Polly panted, "But we got away ... for now."

I nodded, my heart still pounding. "We need to figure out our next move. If Marcella recognized us, she knows we're on to her, and she won't stop until she gets what she wants."

Suddenly, Polly's phone buzzed. She pulled it out, her eyebrows furrowing as she read the message. She looked up at me, a serious expression on her face.

"Lola, Jake says there's been a break-in at the museum," she said, his words dropping like weights.

"Any idea what's missing?"

"Artifacts from the DuPont collection," Polly replied grimly.

"So, Marcella..." I began.

"We can't be sure," Polly interrupted. "But right now, she's our strongest lead. Let's just hope we're not too late."

The pounding bass of my heart drowned out the roar of the engine as I gripped the passenger seat, Polly racing towards the museum at breakneck speed. My mind swirled with thoughts of the cryptic Marcella. Was she behind this? Or did another covet the DuPont treasures?

Polly screeched to a stop in front of a swarm of staff and security, their ashen faces and frantic gestures piercing my chest with dread. Amid the chaos stood Jake, his usual playful smirk replaced by hardened steel. His grave nod in our direction did nothing to calm my nerves.

Polly and I scrambled out of the car, avoiding curious stares, and rushed to Jake's side.

"The DuPont collection ... it's gone." Jake's hushed revelation landed like a sucker punch.

The DuPonts—Worthington's bitter rivals for generations. My eyes locked with Polly's, mirroring the unspoken fear etched into her delicate features.

Jake led us past the once lavish exhibits, now empty shells housing only echoes of their former grandeur. The void left by the pilfered relics conjured images of their tempestuous owner, Brittany DuPont. Her scorn and longing for the rare and beautiful were as renowned as her family's fortune. A picture formed that filled me with dread.

"Does Brittany know?" I dared to ask.

"Not yet." Jake's grim reply offered no comfort.

A tense silence filled the stark chamber as we surveyed the aftermath. The ransacked cabinets and smashed display cases bore evidence of the intruders' reckless haste. As my eyes scanned over the jagged edges of glass littering the floor, a glint of silver caught my eye. Bending down for a closer look, my heart nearly stopped—a lone silver bar lay nestled between the shards, a lone 'M' winking up at me.

I grabbed Polly's arm, unable to tear my eyes from the object. Her sharp intake of breath told me she saw it, too.

"It's Marcella," I whispered. Polly nodded grimly.

"We need to tell Jake," she replied. We made our way to where Jake was speaking with the security staff, taking him aside. Quickly, we told him about the pendant, of the coin we thought may be an old artifact, Marcella in the SUV, and our narrow escape at the barn. His expression grew stern as comprehension dawned.

"Then it's as we feared," Jake said. "Marcella DuPont is behind this. We have to stop her before she makes a bigger mess of things."

A loud commotion at the museum entrance caught our attention. The doors flew open, revealing two figures—a slender woman in an impeccable blue dress, and a burly bodyguard by her side. Even from a distance, Brittany DuPont's commanding presence filled the space.

Her sharp eyes swept over the destruction, as if tallying the missing pieces of her collection. When she landed on us, her eyes narrowed.

"You," she spat, jabbing a finger at Jake. "Explain yourself, and quickly!"

Jake sighed but squared his shoulders, ready to face Brittany's wrath. Before he could speak, however, Brittany held up a hand.

"Never mind, the state of this place tells me enough," she snapped. "My collection—what have you imbeciles done with it? Do you have any idea of its worth?"

"Mrs. DuPont, my apologies," Jake began. "There's been a break-in. Your collection was stolen, we believe by—"

"Stolen?" Brittany shrieked. "How could this happen under your incompetent watch?" She took a threatening step toward Jake, oblivious to her bodyguard's attempts to hold her back.

"It was Marcella!" I blurted out before I could stop myself. All eyes turned to me, stunned into silence by my outburst. I felt Polly's warning nudge but stood my ground.

Brittany glowered at me, cobalt eyes flashing. "Marcella? What nonsense is this?"

I opened my mouth to respond, but I faltered under her icy stare. Polly quickly stepped in, explaining about the barn, the clues we found, and witnessing Marcella sneaking into the museum.

Brittany listened in stoic silence, arms folded across her chest. Finally, she sniffed. "As absurd as this tale sounds, it aligns with that woman's delusions of claiming what is rightfully mine. But if it's proof you want, then proof you shall have. Guards!"

At her command, two suited men stepped forward. "Bring Marcella DuPont to me at once. And call the police." The men nodded, promptly exiting to fulfill her orders.

Brittany turned her razor-sharp glare to us once more. "You two would do well not to cross me again. Now get out of my sight!"

We didn't need telling twice. We left the museum and headed back to our car. I glanced at Polly as we drove back into town. "That was certainly an eventful morning."

Polly let out a shaky laugh. "That's one way to put it. I have to admit, confronting Brittany DuPont was rather terrifying. But at least we got some answers."

"Did we?" I asked. "I feel like we've only uncovered more questions. About Marcella, about the rivalry between the families ... and about Jake."

Polly's brow furrowed, her unspoken question hanging between us. I sighed. "There's something Jake's not telling us. His history with the Worthingtons, his insight into Victor's behavior ... it seems too convenient. I want to trust him, but..."

"You're worried his motives aren't entirely pure," Polly finished. I nodded.

"Then we need to keep digging," she said decisively. "Into Marcella, into Brittany, and into Jake's past. There are secrets here, and lives may depend on us uncovering them."

Her words ignited a spark inside me. As reckless as it seemed, part of me thrilled at the prospect of solving this mystery that had ensnared us. "Where do we start?"

"The DuPont estate. There must be records, documents about its history. Tax records, photographs, letters—anything we can get our hands on. Some clue as to why Marcella chose now to resurface."

I nodded, following her line of thought. "And we look into the Worthington-DuPont feud. There's resentment and rivalry there that goes back generations."

"Exactly. And we find out more about Jake's heritage, his connections to both families. His motivations may not be as straightforward as they seem." Polly sighed, her eyes gleaming with determination. "This won't be without danger. But we've come this far, there's no turning back now."

"Where do we start?" I asked again, feeling invigorated.

Polly smiled, a hint of mischief in her eyes. "I believe the local library has records on the county's older estates and families. Including newspaper clippings, public documents... It's a trove of information if we dig deep enough. Shall we pay them a visit?"

Chapter 9

The library was dim and musty, filled with the comforting smell of old books. We waved at the librarian as we hurried past the front desk. As Polly and I entered the local records room, preparing to dig into the history of the Worthington-DuPont feud, we were startled at what we saw. Books and papers littered the floor, cabinets had been left hanging open. The records we sought had been ransacked with all the care and precision of a toddler let loose in a china shop.

A fine film of dust covered every surface, as if some industrious spider had spun cobwebs across the entire room. Clearly, no one had disturbed this back room in a very long time. Or cleaned it, for that matter,

My heart dropped at the sight of the destruction. "Who could have done this?" I asked in dismay. These documents had stood undisturbed for decades. What were they searching for—and did they find it?

Polly and I set to work reorganizing the records, searching for any clues left behind. For hours, we pored over property records, newspaper clippings, letters—any fragments that remained. Our search, now even more urgent. Surrounded by stacks of records on the Worthington and DuPont families, we looked for any clues that might shed light on the bitter feud between the two dynasties.

"Did you know property disputes could be this riveting?" I asked Polly, stifling a yawn over the eighth straight page of 'Lot 4, west half.'

"I can barely contain my excitement," she replied drily. "Though I may need to grab another coffee to fuel the thrill of it all."

As I skimmed yet another stack of papers, a headline caught my eye: "Mysterious Fire Ravages Worthington Museum Wing." The date at the top of the clipping read July 17th, 1965.

Huh.

"Polly, look at this," I said, sliding the article across the table. Her eyes widened as she read, her face growing pale.

"A fire destroyed the east wing of the Worthington Museum in the early hours of Thursday morning," she read aloud. "While the cause remains unknown, officials estimate nearly half the museum's collection was lost in the blaze. The Worthington family has offered a substantial reward for any information regarding the fire."

Polly looked up at me, realization dawning on her face. "1965 ... that would have been when Jake's grandfather, Elias, was in charge of the museum. Do you think ... could he have been involved, seeking revenge against the Worthingtons?"

My mind raced, piecing together the implications. "It's possible. Losing half the collection would have been devastating. And if there was already resentment towards the Worthingtons..."

"This could explain why Jake has been so eager to help," Polly said. "He may feel responsible, wanting to make things right. But confronting his family's dark history won't be easy." She sighed, resting her chin in her hands. "No wonder this feud has lasted so long. The damage runs deep on both sides."

I nodded, feeling a rush of sympathy for Jake. His motivations were becoming clear, even if his methods remained questionable. The thorny roots of the rivalry had entangled both families for generations.

A vibration in my pocket shook me from my thoughts. I pulled out my phone to find a message from Thomas, the café's clumsy yet well-meaning new employee, requesting I call him right away. His voice sounded strange when he picked up, tense and hushed.

"Thomas, is everything alright?" I asked, pulse quickening with dread. In the background, I could hear shouts from various voices.

"I'm so sorry, I've made a right mess of things," Thomas began, his words spilling out in a rush. "Some thugs showed up, demanding money, and I got so nervous I dropped a whole tray of dishes. Then I gave them what was in the register without thinking."

My hands clenched the phone, imagining the disaster zone the café must have descended into. What trouble had Thomas's clumsiness caused this time? "Did anyone get hurt?" I asked, fearing the worst.

"Everyone's fine, just a bit of a fright," he replied, relief in his voice. At least there was that. "I've called the police already. I'm really sorry for the trouble."

I breathed a sigh of relief, anger already beginning to fade. As exasperating as Thomas could be, I couldn't stay mad at him for long. He meant no harm.

"Lock the doors and keep everyone inside until the police come," I instructed. "We'll be there shortly to help sort things out."

By the time we arrived, the whirlwind Thomas had stirred up was mostly passed—though evidence remained in the form of smashed dishes, scattered coins, and frightened guests. I reassured our customers as Polly helped Thomas mop up the mess in the kitchen.

Jake burst through the doors not long after, face creased with worry. "I came as soon as I heard. Is everyone alright?" His eyes swept over the disarray, then landed on me, heavy with unspoken emotion. I gave a small nod of reassurance and his shoulders sagged with relief.

The remainder of the afternoon passed in a blur of cleanup and paperwork with the officers on the scene. At last, the café emptied out, leaving just Polly, Jake, and me slumped around a table as twilight descended. The day's discoveries and disasters had left me feeling drained, yet determined.

Jake's swift arrival nagged at me as the day wound down. How did he know about the incident at the café so quickly? I had only just called Thomas myself, and it took us some time to arrive from the library.

Yet he had come rushing over the moment there was trouble, concern etched deep in his face. It was as if he had known the danger we were in before it arose.

As Jake helped stack chairs, I studied his profile, trying to reconcile the different sides of him I had seen. He could be charming and sympathetic one moment, then evasive and manipulative the next. His motivations and intentions remained shrouded in mystery.

I shook off the thought, reminding myself his true motives were still unclear. Still, his swift appearance after the confrontation with those thugs felt off. I made a mental note to press him for more details when the opportunity arose.

Polly broke the silence first. "Those thugs today might have been upset with the Worthingtons and took it out on the wrong place. We could have gotten caught in the crossfire of their feud."

I bristled at the thought, at how little control we had over forces that might descend upon us at any time. We had to do something to end this, for our own safety and for everyone else in this town.

My eyes fell on Jake, hands curled around a cup of tea, gazing into its depths as if it held answers. "We found something at the library today that might explain why your family has been so eager to make amends."

Chapter 10

J ake looked up, his expression guarded. "What did you find?"

I took a deep breath, steadying my nerves. "Records indicating your grandfather may have started the museum fire of 1965 to seek revenge against the Worthingtons."

Jake stared at me, stunned. The cup slipped from his hands, clattering against the table. "My grandfather blamed the Worthingtons for losing everything in the Great Depression. He always said they took advantage of others." Pain flickered in his eyes. "The threatening notes sent to the Worthingtons before the fire ... it all makes sense now. The hatred was always there, simmering beneath the surface."

Jake's face tightened as he read the article. It claimed the fire had been started deliberately, and the museum director, Elias Harvey DuPont—Jake's grandfather—was the primary suspect. Threatening notes had been found, apparently written by Elias.

"Is your grandfather still alive?" I asked gently.

Jake shook his head. "He died when I was fifteen. Took the truth behind his anger with him to the grave. And his secret BBQ sauce recipe, much to my everlasting chagrin."

I reached across the table, grasping his hand. "I'm so sorry. We'll find answers together."

At last Jake spoke, his voice strained. "My grandfather... He never said a word about the fire." Pain flickered in his eyes. "My grandfather always blamed Worthington for ruining our family. He said Worthington was a thief who stole credit for his work." Jake met my eyes, pain flickering in his eyes. "But I never thought he would take such drastic action for revenge."

"We don't have the full truth yet." Though pieces were falling into place, the entire picture remained obscured.

"Lola, I want you to know—I had nothing to do with this—"

Before I could respond, a small explosion shook the table, smoke quickly filling the café. My heart leaped into my throat as I searched for the source. To my relief, I spied Thomas waving a fire extinguisher at the oven, which was belching clouds of smoke.

"I'm so sorry!" he cried. "I was trying to bake scones as a surprise, but I fear I've made rather a mess of things."

We gaped at Thomas in disbelief. How on earth had he caused such chaos when we thought he left hours ago?

Jake was the first to laugh, tension broken by the absurdity of the situation.

Thomas flushed, stumbling over his feet.

I sighed, pulse gradually slowing. How ever did Thomas manage to stir up disaster even when attempting to help in secret? His attempts at help seemed destined to end in calamity.

Thomas ducked his head, embarrassed by the trouble he had stirred up yet again. "I'm so sorry. Oh, my gosh. I'll just close up and bid you all goodnight." He tripped over his own feet in his haste to exit.

Jake ran a hand through his hair, eyes distant. The momentary alarm had disrupted our conversation, scattering thoughts and emotions left raw and exposed.

"Perhaps we should continue this tomorrow, when we've had time to process," I said tentatively. Darkness had fully descended outside, weariness creeping into my bones. We had uncovered much today, though answers remained elusive as the shadows that lurked beyond sight.

Jake nodded. "For now, we should get some rest. But this isn't over yet—not by a long shot." His eyes gleamed with a restless energy that told me sleep would not come easily for him tonight. "Tomorrow, we visit Marcella. She's the key to unraveling this whole sordid affair."

Apprehension twisted in my gut at the thought of facing Marcella DuPont again. Memories of our last encounter flashed in my mind. The barn, the SUV barreling towards us, the near miss. Her silk smile and honeyed words concealed fangs beneath, ready to strike at any threat to her gilded existence. "Are you certain that's wise? She nearly ran us over at the barn to cover her tracks, and won't give up secrets easily. We'll never get the truth from her, Jake."

Jake brushed off my concerns with a wave of his hand. "We have to try. Don't worry, I can handle Marcella DuPont. The police questioned her about the museum break-in, but she slipped through their fingers. She won't slip through mine."

His confidence did little to quell the doubts swirling within me. Marcella was accustomed to getting her way in all things and wouldn't take kindly to anyone standing in the path of her desires.

The next morning dawned cold and gray as Jake and I made our way to Marcella's estate, a sprawling neoclassical mansion set on sculpted grounds. As I stared up at the imposing façade, a shiver of foreboding ran down my spine. Somewhere behind the pristine white columns and elaborately curtained windows, Marcella was lying in wait, ready to spin her web of deception.

In my pocket, I felt the weight of the coins we had found at the barn. It was a reminder of Marcella's potential for harm. As we approached her mansion, I took one out, rolling it between my fingers.

"This is a mistake," I said, clutching Jake's arm. "Marcella is too cunning. We'll never get a straight answer from her."

Jake brushed aside my worries, confident in his ability to outmaneuver her wiles.

Marcella greeted us at the massive oak door, a vision of charm in silk and diamonds, as always. "Welcome to Thornfield!" She acted as though she had been expecting us. We were ushered into the foyer, a grand staircase sweeping up to a gallery above dominated the area, and magnificent marble floors were gleaming under crystal chandeliers. The trappings of old wealth and status were on full display, each piece of artwork and furnishing carefully selected to convey prestige.

"It's just like the barn," I murmured to Jake. "Only this time, we aren't the ones being hunted. It's the truth we are after."

"May I offer you tea in the solarium? The view of the gardens is splendid." Marcella glided ahead without waiting for a response, slippers on her feet making no sound.

We followed her into a glass-walled room drenched with sunlight, exotic plants, and flowers in full bloom. Servants silently appeared with tea and refreshments on silver trays before melting away as quietly as they came. Marcella reclined into a wicker chair, rings sparkling as she gestured gracefully for us to sit.

Jake nodded courteously. "Ms. DuPont. We have a few questions, if you don't mind."

I studied Jake as he spoke, searching for any cracks in his polished demeanor. His history with the Worthingtons and DuPonts was proving increasingly murky. What stake did he have in uncovering the truth, and could his motives be as pure as they seemed?

"Of course, have some refreshments first!" Marcella, her smile never wavering. As we poured some tea and gathered a few finger sandwiches, I felt the same chill I had felt back in the barn. Just like Marcella's beam from the spotlight scanning the barn, Marcella's eyes swept over us now. It was a chilling reminder of what we were up against. The lavish furnishings and artwork on display spoke of old money and influence.

"Okay, now, how may I assist you?"

Jake cleared his throat, measuring his words. "We hoped to ask you a bit more about Worthington's passing. And your involvement with threats against our family prior to the museum fire."

Marcella blinked, angling her head. "Threats and fires? I'm afraid I don't follow. My charity work keeps me rather occupied, you see." She gave a tinkling laugh, patting Jake's hand. "You must have me mistaken for someone else. I don't even own a lighter."

Jake pressed on, undeterred. "Did Worthington's death secured your lifestyle and estates for the foreseeable future with money coming your way from his estate?. And the fire destroyed half of the family's collection, nearly ruining us." His eyes were steel, seeing through her charade. "A striking coincidence, wouldn't you say?"

Marcella sighed, toying with a pearl necklace. "While Worthington's passing was tragic, I had nothing to gain from it. My charity foundations provide ample means of income, and as for the family's misfortunes..." She waved a hand airily. "I was merely a young socialite at the time. It's my family too. Why would I want to destroy precious art and the museum for that matter? I've no notion of any threats or damage done, though I am dreadfully sorry to think that you believe I had anything to do with it."

Her lies slid off her tongue with ease, not a trace of deception visible. But underneath the polished veneer, I sensed a cunning ruthlessness that would allow nothing to threaten her gilded world. Marcella had played the game too long, the lure of status and control her greatest motivations.

Jake sat back, jaw clenched in frustration. Marcella stared at him with pity, her mask flawlessly intact. "I do hope you find the truth and closure you're seeking. But I'm afraid I can provide no insights, as these affairs of vengeance and suspicion are outside the realm of my experiences."

Rising gracefully, Marcella drifted to the door. "Now if you'll excuse me, I must prepare to chair a fundraiser this evening. Do give my regards to Brittany when you see her at the museum." The door clicked shut behind us with an air of finality, Marcella slipping through our grasp like the phantom we sought in vain.

Chapter 11

I stretched, muscles aching from tension and lack of sleep. After leaving Thornfield, doubts and worries had plagued me through the night. Marcella DuPont's venomous smile seared into my memory.

A soft knock sounded at the door. "Are you awake?" Polly peeked in, concern etched on her face. "How did it go yesterday?"

I sighed, pushing stray hairs from my eyes. "It was … unproductive. Marcella evaded our questions and we're no closer to answers."

Polly sat on the edge of the bed, lifting my rabbit Tetley into her lap. He nuzzled into her hand, searching for treats and attention. "You two need a day off from sleuthing. Some time in nature and fresh country air will do you good."

I smiled at Tetley, warmth flooding through me. "You may be right. And speaking of nature, we should take Tetley for his checkup at the vet today."

Polly grinned, passing Tetley to me. "Perfect. A day with the bunny doctor it is."

The drive to the vet took us through winding country roads, sunlight dappling through dense forest on either side. By the time we arrived at the little red cottage that housed the vet's office, a sense of peace had settled over me.

Dr. Mendel greeted us warmly, ushering us into the examination room. "And how is our favorite patient today?" He lifted Tetley from his carrier, fingers gently probing his ears and paws. Tetley relaxed into his hands, munching on a treat.

"He's been quite well," I said. "Eating hearty and keeping us on our toes. Has he gained enough weight?"

Dr. Mendel nodded, jotting notes on a chart. "Tetley looks very healthy. His coat is glossy, teeth are in good shape, and he's at an ideal weight." He handed Tetley a carrot stick, watching him nibble away happily.

Dr. Mendel smiled and continued to jot. But as his hands ran over Tetley's side, he paused. A small frown creased his brow.

"Is something wrong?" Alarm trickled down my spine. Our quiet day was about to take an unexpected turn.

Dr. Mendel sighed, removing his glasses. "I felt a small lump on Tetley's right side that concerns me. It could be nothing, but to be safe, I'd like to do a quick biopsy."

My heart sank as Dr. Mendel prepared a needle. Tetley remained still, chewing placidly on his carrot stick without protest as the sample was taken.

Polly squeezed my hand, offering a reassuring smile. "I'm sure it's just a false alarm. Tetley seems perfectly content." But her words did little to assuage the worry churning within me.

Mysteries clung to us, it seemed, even on a day meant for escaping troubles.

Dr. Mendel glanced down at Tetley thoughtfully, eyes shadowed behind wire-rimmed glasses. "The results will take a few days. Try not to worry—the odds are good that the lump is simply a benign growth."

I swallowed hard, struggling to rein in my anxiety as reality crashed over me. "A few days? Can't you examine the sample now to determine if it's dangerous?"

Dr. Mendel shook his head, expression grave yet kind. "I understand your concern. However, a proper biopsy analysis requires time and resources I do not have access to here." He gave Tetley an affectionate scratch on the head, eliciting a contented purr. "For now, keep a close eye on this little fellow. Watch for changes in appetite or behavior and notify me right away if anything seems amiss."

Numbness spread through me as we drove home under leaden skies, Tetley dozing in my lap without a care. I stared down at his soft white fur, heart constricting at the thought of losing my faithful companion. He had been Uncle Iggy's companion and became mine after he was murdered. Tetley had seen me through every turbulent chapter since. A life without Tetley was one left hollow and bereft of warmth.

Polly glanced over, sensing my distress. "You heard what Dr. Mendel said. The odds are in Tetley's favor. And he shows no signs of distress or ill health." Her fingers found mine, giving a comforting squeeze. "Try to stay optimistic. I'm sure the test results will provide reassurance that this is just a scare."

I stroked Tetley's ears half-heartedly. "Optimism has never come easily. You know that." My thoughts strayed to the troubling questions still surrounding us. A wave of exhaustion washing over me. "Some days, it seems the world is determined to heap loss and heartache at every turn. I don't think I could bear Tetley being taken too."

Polly blinked hard, eyes glistening. "Then let's make the most of right now. No sense worrying over what may never come to pass." She turned the radio on, filling the silence. " We'll have a movie marathon, bake cinnamon rolls, spoil this little fur ball rotten. The troubles of tomorrow can wait."

After settling Tetley into his bed with treats and fresh water, I retreated to the balcony and pulled out my phone with shaking hands. The line rang twice before a familiar voice answered, rough yet gentle.

"Lola? Is everything alright?" Harry's tone was caught between greeting and concern. I blinked back tears, clutching the phone like a lifeline.

"Harry, I ... we took Tetley to the vet today. They found a lump and did a biopsy. The results won't be back for days, and I'm just..." My voice trailed off as anguish threatened to overcome me.

Harry was silent for a long moment. "I see. That is worrisome news." He let out a heavy sigh, regret clear in his tone. "I wish I was there to offer you comfort in person. Tetley is a fighter, you know that."

I squeezed my eyes shut, allowing his soothing words to wash over me. No matter storms that arose between us, Harry remained my shelter from every tempest. "Harry," I whispered, trying to stifle the lump in my throat. "Can you come over? I could use some company."

A pause, then, "Lola, I'd be there in a heartbeat if I could. You know that." His voice was quiet, and I could hear the regret lacing his words. "I'm at a crucial point in a case. But if things ease up..."

His words hung in the air, a promise unfulfilled. A part of me knew I was asking too much, but the hurt was too raw. "Alright," I managed to say, though my disappointment was evident.

"I'm sorry, Lola," Harry murmured, and his voice was so tender it threatened to break me. "I promise we'll catch up soon. Try to get some rest, alright? And give Tetley a pat for me."

"I will," I replied, a little stronger now. "Thank you, Harry."

I ended the call, staring at the screen for a moment before slipping the phone back into my pocket. When I turned around, Polly was standing in the doorway. Her eyes were soft, understanding.

"He couldn't make it?" she asked gently, already knowing the answer.

I shook my head, the disappointment a bitter taste on my tongue. "He's caught up in a case."

Polly sighed, stepping onto the balcony and closing the distance between us. She didn't say anything, didn't need to. Her presence was comforting enough.

"Let's make some tea," she suggested after a while, her voice bright despite the circumstances. "And how about we start on those cinnamon rolls? Tetley could use some spoiling, don't you think?"

I nodded, the ghost of a smile tugging at my lips. "Sounds good. And maybe we can pick a movie? Something light?"

"Perfect," Polly agreed, her smile echoing mine. "A cozy night in, just what we need."

We settled into the rhythm of the evening, Tetley snuggled on a cushion between us as we watched a movie, lost in a world of laughter and light. The scent of cinnamon rolls wafted from the kitchen, a promise of comfort.

As the night drew on, we were startled by a knock on the door. I looked at Polly, puzzled. We weren't expecting anyone.

"Who could that be at this hour?" she murmured, glancing at the clock.

I rose, heart pounding as I moved to the door. The hall was dim; the light casting a faint glow as I peered through the peephole, and my breath hitched.

"Harry," I breathed out, swinging the door open.

He stood there with a concerned look etched on his face. "Lola, I was able to wrap up the crucial part of the case earlier than expected. I didn't want you to face this night alone. Is it too late to offer some company?"

A warm, tearful laugh escaped me. Relief washed over like a summer rain, a soothing balm to my frayed nerves. "It's never too late, Harry. Thank you."

Polly appeared behind me, her eyes wide with surprise. "Harry? This is a pleasant surprise."

"Hello, Polly." He smiled, stepping inside. "I'm sorry for the late visit. I wanted to make sure Lola and Tetley are alright."

"Of course, it's never too late," Polly reassured, moving aside to let Harry in. He looked every bit the detective, even off duty. His clothes were casual yet stylish, a departure from the standard uniform he often wore. Yet his demeanor, a blend of self-assuredness and persistent determination, betrayed his profession.

As he stepped into the living room, Tetley immediately perked up. The little rabbit had an uncanny ability to sense the mood in the room, and the unexpected arrival of Harry had him alert and curious.

Harry crouched down to pet Tetley, his rugged hands gentle as they stroked the rabbit's soft fur. His hazel-green eyes softened as he looked at Tetley, a sense of genuine concern evident. "Hello there, brave little fellow. I hear you've been to the doctor today."

I felt a lump form in my throat as I watched Harry and Tetley, the normally rigid detective, showing a tender side that was surprisingly endearing. He was always so sure of himself, so confident in his instincts and judgment. Yet in this moment, he appeared genuine, compassionate even.

Polly gave me a wave and headed down the hallway to her room.

After a while, Harry stood up and turned to face me, his eyes meeting mine. There was an uncharacteristic vulnerability in his dropped eyes, a softness that took me by surprise.

"I know you're worried, Lola," he started, his voice low and comforting. "But remember, Tetley is a fighter, and he has the best care possible. We'll deal with whatever comes, one day at a time."

I managed a small, grateful smile. "Thank you, Harry. I'm glad you're here." My smile faded as I thought of this Worthington situation, a troubling situation that hit close to home. "You said you were able to wrap up a crucial part of a case? What case would that be?"

Harry's expression turned guarded, hazel eyes shadowed. "Ah, yes … that. It was straightforward enough, just time-consuming." Harry sighed, running a hand through his artfully tousled hair. His steel hazel brown eyes met mine reluctantly. "I'm afraid I need to keep the details quiet. Until it is time.

Frustration simmered in me. "And when will that be? After the killer strikes again?" I held his eyes, matching his determination. "I have been hunting clues to help you, Harry. Don't ask me to stand aside now."

Harry's expression hardened. "This isn't a game, Lola. I'm a detective. You own a café. The stakes are too high to risk an amateur mucking things up." His eyes cut to Tetley, a muscle twitching in his jaw. "I won't allow it."

Harry's words stung, a sharp slap of reality. "An amateur mucking things up?" I repeated, voice shaking with indignation. "So that's what you think of me, then? Just a café owner who's out of her depth?"

"That's not what I meant, Lola—" Harry began, but I cut him off, my heart pounding with hurt and anger.

"No, I think I understand perfectly." I met his gaze, challenging him. "You've decided I'm not cut out for this. That I should just go back to serving coffee and baking scones while you handle the 'real' detective work."

Harry ran a hand over his face, frustration creasing his features. "Lola, this isn't about your capabilities. This is about safety. About keeping you—"

I held up a hand, silencing him. "I don't need you to keep me safe, Harry. I need you to respect me. To trust me. And right now? It doesn't feel like you're doing either."

His mouth opened and closed, no words coming out. For once, the eloquent detective seemed at a loss for words. I took a deep breath, centering myself. "I think it would be best if you left, Harry."

His face fell, but he didn't argue. Quietly, he moved toward the door. Before he exited, he turned to me. "Lola, I..." But whatever he was going to say, he seemed to think better of it. With a final, regretful glance my way, he stepped out into the hall, leaving me in the quiet apartment with only my thoughts and Tetley for company.

After the door closed, I slumped back against the wall, my heart aching. I'd been excited when he'd shown up, had felt a rush of relief to see his familiar face. But now, in the wake of our argument, I felt more alone than ever.

Chapter 12

The bell chimed as Jake entered the Gallery Café, sunlight glinting off his dark hair. His eyes met mine, and Jake's face lit up with a grin. I smiled back, though mine quickly faded. Jake strolled over, hands in pockets.

"That gloomy look won't win you any customers. They might think we overdosed the lemonade with lemon juice!"

I rolled my eyes, but grinned at his joke. "Don't you have security guarding to do?"

Jake's grin vanished, his casual manner shifting to concern. "I wanted to check on you. We haven't really talked since our visit to Marcella. Is everything alright?"

I sighed, setting down my cloth forcefully. "Tetley may be sick, and Harry and I had a row."

Jake's eyes softened with understanding. "Do you want to talk about it?"

The pain of Harry's insults and distrust came flooding back, an ache filling my chest. I told Jake all about the events from yesterday and of the exchange Harry and I had, my frustration at being pushed aside. His support and empathy comforted me.

When I finished, Jake sighed. "Harry's a fool not to see you're an asset. I know how much you want to solve this mystery. If you want help investigating, I'm here for anything."

Jake glanced at me, care and determination in his eyes. Part of me wanted to take him up on the offer. There were still too many unanswered questions surrounding the museum and the Worthington-DuPont feud ... and Victor remained suspicious.

"I can access the museum archives. We could find clues to piece together the truth."

A surge of excitement went through me at a possible breakthrough. We made plans to sneak in again tonight.

Adrenaline rushed through me as Jake led us into the museum under cover of night. We descended into the musty basement, flashlight beams slicing through the darkness.

Dusty boxes lined old shelves, files untouched for decades. Cobwebs caught against my skin, a chill running through me.

"Look for anything on the '65 fire or Worthington's deals," Jake said, his hushed voice echoing.

After some time, Polly gasped. "Lola, come look at this!"

My heart raced as I brushed cobwebs aside, following Polly to the shelves where she found the rolled up diagrams. We cleared away dust and debris to get a better look.

"These are the original blueprints for the museum construction," Polly said, excitement rising in her hushed voice. "But look—there's an extra wing sketched here that was never built."

I bent closer, tracing the lines and measurements with my fingertip. She was right. The west wing on these plans was at least twice the size of what had actually been constructed. Why the change? I felt a surge of anticipation at probing into long-held secrets waiting to be revealed.

Jake peered over our shoulders, brow furrowed. He pointed to a narrow space between rooms on the drafts—a space that didn't exist on any public museum map. "Could that be a hidden passageway?"

A secret corridor—what might lie within its shadows, untouched all these years? With another look at the true museum layout, there seemed only one place it could be ... behind the bricked-over fireplace in Gallery 4.

Without consultation, as if sensing the others' thoughts, we swiftly moved across rooms and corridors, arriving breathless at Gallery 4. We found what seemed like the only place this corridor could be. "Wait here." Jake said. He hurried out of the room and was soon back with a toolbox in hand. Jake grabbed a crowbar to pry out bricks, his motions fueled with the same determined curiosity as mine.

With scraping sounds, bricks came loose and fell away. A gap appeared, and then a void of black. Jake shone his flashlight through, revealing a narrow space and dust-covered stairs descending below. A hidden underworld beneath the museum's surface.

Filled with a mixture of anticipation and trepidation, we squeezed single-file through the opening, cobwebs snagging at our hair and clothes. At the foot of the stairs, we found ourselves in a long sealed-off room. Our lights exposed a clutter of objects: furniture, canvas-draped shapes, a large cabinet.

My eyes widened as we approached the crates, each one bearing the initials "J.W."—Joseph Worthington.

The tension hung heavy in the air as I carefully pried open the first crate. As the lid came off, my eyes widened at the sight of stacks of old letters and files within. I gingerly pulled out a handful, my hands trembling slightly as I blew off the old layer of dust and ash.

"The letters ... they are between Worthington and Victor DuPont," I managed to utter, the words catching in my throat. The room fell silent, the only sound the rustling of paper as I flipped through the documents. The damning details of their clandestine deal unfolded before us, a twisted narrative that none of us expected.

I paused for a moment, letting the implications of what we'd found sink in. It wasn't just a property negotiation; there were scandalous photos, hinting at something darker. "These ... these are blackmail files," I said, my voice a hushed whisper. "Victor is in these photos ... in compromising and unlawful situations."

I felt the room spin slightly as we processed this revelation. This was a motive, a potential reason for Victor to want Worthington out of the way. But was it enough to drive him to murder? Despite the evidence we had uncovered, I wasn't entirely convinced.

Just as we were digesting this new information, Jake was already prying open another crate. His movements were slow, deliberate. As he opened it, he paused, eyes widening. "There's more," he said, his voice barely above a whisper.

Jake slowly pulled out a leather-bound journal, its cover worn with age. "Worthington's personal diary," he confirmed, flipping open the cover. He carefully turned the pages, eyes skimming the handwritten notes.

A sudden change in Jake's expression caught my attention. His eyes grew wide, his brows furrowing in disbelief. "The last entry ... it's dated just before his death."

Jake fell silent, his eyes glued to the pages. Polly and I exchanged glances, our breath hitching as we waited for him to share the contents. The air seemed to grow denser, the weight of the upcoming revelation making my heart pound in my chest.

"What is it?" Polly and I cried in unison. Jake looked up from the journal, his expression unreadable.

He took a deep breath before uttering the words that would change everything.

"The foolish boy thinks his threats frighten me. As if I would hand the museum over now, when my greatest triumph is in reach ... the prize I've awaited for years under their oblivious noses. Let Victor act out his petty vengeance; none shall stop me now from claiming what is mine ... the diamond Necklace of Transylvanian royalty, thought lost forever but soon to sparkle around the neck of my dear—"

Jake's voice cut off abruptly. "It's not Victor," he rasped. "Worthington had an accomplice ... a woman he was romancing. She's the real killer."

He looked at the journal again, his brows furrowing. "There's more here ... let me read it."

Jake started reading again: "... the diamond Necklace of Transylvanian royalty, thought lost forever but soon to sparkle around the neck of my dear Brittany."

Chapter 13

Brittany DuPont and Joseph Worthington had been seeing each other. This shocking twist called everything we knew into question. Jake mumbled, "I always thought she had better taste."

Jake closed the diary, confusion etched on his face. "Brittany accused Marcella so quickly to avoid exposing her own guilt. If she and Worthington were lovers, she had more motive than anyone to want him silenced."

My mind raced, reevaluating each encounter with Brittany. Maybe her bold rivalry had been a front to disguise their forbidden affair? Sure, she seemed cold and cunning, but I supposed even someone like Brittany DuPont had a humanity we'd underestimated. And if Worthington betrayed her, then her thirst for vengeance would know no bounds.

"We have to find evidence linking them," I said, glancing at Jake, our eyes meeting for a moment longer than necessary. "Search the diary for clues about their relationship. I'll go through the photos again—unless you fancy doing that together?"

He flashed me a grin. "Sure."

We set to work as more pieces fell into place. Hmm, I thought, running over everything that had happened so far in my mind. *The hidden door in Brittany's garden may have been an old rendezvous point. And if Worthington gave her the Necklace of Transylvanian Royalty during their affair, her desire to keep this secret would provide motive to silence him.*

How much of this could I trust Jake with? I took a leap.

"We have to investigate Brittany's estate for more clues," I said. "That hidden door Polly photographed could lead somewhere revealing."

"Good thinking partner!"

Partner?

I saw Polly silently smirk, but she said nothing.

The night air was crisp as we slipped under cover of darkness toward the hidden door in Brittany's garden. Our flashlight beams cut through a tangle of vines and branches obscuring the weathered door.

Jake pried at the weathered door with a crowbar until it creaked open. A musty passage led us down rickety steps into a cellar. "Well, this isn't ominous at all," he said, trying to lighten the mood. "Just your typical secret basement beneath a perfectly normal garden."

"Stay close," Jake whispered.

Our lights slid over gardening tools and supplies before landing on a locked metal door.

"This is no potting shed," Jake said. "Help me find a key, Lola, or we'll have to break in."

We rummaged through drawers until Polly plucked out an old key. It slid into the lock, clicking open to reveal a hidden room filled with paintings and artifacts.

My own eyes fell upon a familiar canvas—one of the rare paintings Worthington had snatched up, according to Jake's research. But how did it end up here? I spotted a painting of Worthington in his younger days—had Brittany kept it out of lingering affection or resentment?

A noise sounded above. Footsteps! We froze, panic locking our eyes. "Turn off the light!" Jake hissed.

We scrambled behind the door as the cellar steps creaked open. Through a crack, lamplight flickered on Brittany, scanning the area with narrowed eyes.

My pulse raced as she entered, locking the door behind her. We held our breath until the light faded and her footsteps retreated.

Jake turned the flashlight back on, his hand brushing against mine as he did, a spark of connection momentarily distracting us. "We better get out of here before she returns. Although, I must say, the thought of getting caught with you does have its thrills."

I laughed nervously, the adrenaline from our narrow escape mixing with the unexpected warmth of his compliment. "Flirting in the face of danger, Jake? You're a unique breed."

I saw Polly roll her eyes.

His eyes glimmered for a second, but his jaw tightened as he refocused on the situation at hand. "But this proves Brittany's hiding something—maybe even evidence linking her to Worthington's murder."

"Not so fast, amateur sleuths." We whirled to find Brittany gazing at us, eyes piercing, yet weary. Strands of hair escaped her chignon, betraying distress despite her styled appearance. She sighed. "So—you found my secrets at last. I suppose the truth must come out now."

Uh-oh. This was definitely a compromising position. And there was nowhere to run—except into further danger. I pressed a little closer into Jake than I intended to. His heart was beating just about as quickly as mine was.

Brittany's eyes flashed with anger and regret. "You've outdone your-selves. I commend your persistence, however misguided." My heart sank. Were we still in the dark after coming this far?

Jake spoke up. "We found the hidden room, Brittany. And the paintings that didn't belong to you. Do you have anything to say before we add 'theft' to the charges?"

Brittany sighed again, sorrow etched into her features. Her stare held mine, and in a voice laden with regret, she began unraveling the tangled truth at last.

Brittany's eyes flickered over the paintings in the hidden room, a mix of sadness and defiance in her eyes. "Yes, I did a little redecorating," she admitted, a hint of humor threading her voice. "But it wasn't about the thrill of being an art thief. These pieces were part of my history with Joseph Worthington, a bit like love letters in oil paint."

I shot a glance at Jake in the dark, but I couldn't tell if he was buying this either.

She took a deep breath, her eyes momentarily distant as she relived memories of the past. "Joe and I, we were like two peas in an odd, art-obsessed pod. When our relationship ended, I couldn't bear to see them hanging all smug in the museum, taunting me with what we once had. So, I rehomed them here, in this secret room, away from the prying eyes of art critics and curious minds."

Brittany's voice took on an edge of defiance, belaying the vulnera-bility beneath her steely demeanor. "I never intended to sell or profit from these paintings. They're like my secret stash of chocolate—just less fattening. They were a part of my heart, a testament to the love

Joseph and I shared. But I didn't kill him. Oh, I was furious, and hurt by his betrayal. But wishing him dead? I never wanted him to die."

We stood in tense silence, digesting Brittany's explanation. Her eyes flickered between defiance and vulnerability as she waited for our reaction. I pulled away from Jake a little. The cool air in this cellar hit me. Being pressed up against him wasn't so bad, I supposed.

Jake was the first to speak. "Okay, Brittany — You say you never wished Worthington dead, yet you accused Marcella so quickly. Why divert suspicion from yourself if you have nothing to hide?"

Brittany sighed. "I suspected Marcella because she was always jealous of Joseph and me. But killing him would gain her nothing. It would only hurt her with him not around to give her hush money about us. I see now I was too quick to judge in my grief."

Her words seemed sincere, yet doubts still lingered. "If Worthington betrayed you, your anger could have led to vengeance," I said.

Pain flashed in Brittany's eyes. "Joseph broke my heart, but I could never take his life. I loved him despite everything—as I will always love him, even now he's gone."

"Yet you hid these paintings to erase reminders of your relationship," Jake said. "Rather than cherish your memories as you claim."

Brittany's lips pressed into a bitter smile. "The heart is complicated, Mr. Harvey. I couldn't stand the sight of Joseph, but still longed for him. The paintings were all I had left, so I locked them away where only I could see them."

Her words resonated with sorrow and conflicted emotion. But was this the full truth, or a means to gain our sympathy?

"Please, show us the rest of this room so we may determine your innocence," I said.

We searched the remaining crates but found little aside from dust and cobwebs. My heart, however, skipped a beat when my eyes landed on a small, gold locket lying almost hidden in a dusty corner. I recalled seeing it before, or at least its picture. Worthington had displayed it in one of his exhibits, claiming it was a gift from a Russian Tsar to his mistress. The locket had disappeared from the museum soon after, causing a minor scandal.

I picked up the locket, brushing off the dust, and showed it to Jake. "Remember this from Worthington's Russian collection? It vanished from the museum soon after the exhibition."

Jake's eyes widened as he examined the locket. "Yes, I remember," he murmured. "If this is the same locket, it could mean that Brittany was involved in ... more than just the theft of some paintings."

Brittany, watching our exchange, seemed to lose some of her color. She glanced at the locket, as if seeing it for the first time. "That belonged to Joseph," she said, her voice hardly audible. "I had forgotten it was here."

Her reaction seemed more than just forgetfulness. Had the sight of Worthington's locket stirred memories she would rather have left buried? My doubts, which had faded, came rushing back.

"If this locket was Worthington's, why do you have it?" I asked. "What else in here belonged to him?"

Brittany opened her mouth, but no words came out. In the lengthening silence, Jake pried open a locked cabinet. At once, Brittany's poise shattered.

"Those were from long ago ... please, they're private..." she pleaded upon seeing the contents.

Jake scanned the letters, his brow furrowing. "These suggest Worthington still harbored affection for you ... and resentment toward Marcella. Yet there are hints he tired of your 'possessiveness' in recent months."

"What are you implying?" Brittany demanded.

"Simply that Worthington's betrayal may have cut deeper than you admit," Jake said. "Deep enough to drive you to retaliate in anger."

"You know nothing of my relationship with Joseph!" Brittany cried. "I loved him until the end, as wretched and deceitful as he was. He broke my heart, but I would never have harmed him!"

Her outburst was a slip in her composure.

Departing Brittany's mini Versailles, I think we all agreed on two things: we needed to gather our thoughts, and we were starving. I think we all needed a moment to shake off the cloak-and-dagger vibes, not to mention the dust. Nothing like an all-night diner to shift gears from solving murder mysteries to arguing over the merits of blueberry versus apple pie.

We slid into a booth, the day's events still swirling in our minds. After leaving Brittany's estate, we knew a late-night meeting was in order to review the clues and determine our next steps.

The waitress poured mugs of coffee and left us with menus as we pondered the revelations of the evening. I broke the contemplative silence first.

"Do you think Brittany was telling the truth about keeping the paintings out of sentiment?"

Jake sighed, brow furrowed. "Part of me wants to believe her. But finding those old letters suggests the ending of their relationship may have cut deeper than she admits. And her reaction upon seeing them ..."

"Seemed more than just longing for pleasant memories," I finished. Jake nodded.

"If Brittany did kill Worthington, she's covered her tracks well," Polly said. "Aside from the paintings, we found little evidence in that room. But there could be more clues on the estate should we keep investigating."

"I keep coming back to her accusation of Marcella," Jake said. "It seemed a ploy to divert suspicion, making her reaction all the more telling. But then again, perhaps she truly was mistaken in her grief..."

We were quiet again, turning over each new clue and contradiction in our minds. The waitress delivered slices of pie and refilled our mugs before Jake voiced another thought.

"Even if Brittany didn't kill him... Do you think Worthington's paying off Marcella could have angered her enough to retaliate in another way? Was that all he was doing? Paying to keep her quiet?"

The theory struck me as plausible. While Brittany claimed enduring love for Worthington, hints of anger and jealousy towards Marcella had emerged. Could her desire to harm a romantic rival have led to vengeance, even if she didn't intend murder?

Chapter 14

I stifled a yawn, craving the solitude of the early morning and a strong cup of coffee.

As the rich, earthy aroma of freshly brewed coffee wafted through the kitchen, my phone rang, jolting me from my contemplative silence. Seeing Jake's name on the caller ID brought a mix of anticipation and uncertainty. Our undeniable chemistry the night before had left me torn between a desire for more and a fear of history repeating itself.

As if bracing myself for a cold swim, I took a lungful of air, filling my lungs with courage before I accepted the call. "Good morning," I greeted, hoping my voice didn't betray my nerves.

"I just had a craving for another slice of that diner's apple pie," Jake replied with what sounded like a grin in his voice. "And a growing desire for your charming company again, preferably without the threat of hidden rooms looming over us. What would you say to a private tour of the museum's latest Egyptian exhibit tonight instead? I can arrange access after public hours."

My pulse quickened at the thought of an entire evening lost in history with Jake. And yet, doubt whispered of past heartbreak. I took a breath to steady my voice. "The museum sounds lovely, as long as you promise no mysteries or stakeouts tonight."

Jake laughed. "You have my word. No mysteries, just a quiet evening together surrounded by artifacts of the ancient world. Meet me in front of the museum at eight?"

With the link between our sleuthing and personal time now severed, I found my enthusiasm for the date building. "It's a plan. See you at eight."

The museum loomed before me, shadowed and still. I checked my watch, chiding myself for arriving early in my nervousness. After a few minutes, Jake emerged, cap in place, to escort me inside.

"Welcome to your private tour, mademoiselle," Jake grinned, offering his arm with an exaggerated bow.

I swept into an equally exaggerated curtsy. "Why thank you, kind sir! Please, regale me with tales of ancient treasures and adventure."

As we wandered the Egyptian wing, Jake's knowledge of each artifact amazed me. I found myself leaning into his side, lost in tales of pharaohs and gods.

In the next gallery, I nearly tripped over a stray box left in the walkway. "Two left feet," I joked, my uneasy chuckle echoing off the walls. My unease grew. Was this date a trick to keep me here after hours for some sinister reason? Yet in the European paintings, Jake stared softly at me with open admiration. My doubts seemed foolish.

As we headed to the exit of the room, other voices echoed close by. Jake stopped to listen, thinking it was probably just the guards on duty.

The voices rose in anger, moving closer. "You told us you knew where the diamond was. You said this was a foolproof plan. Take us to it now!"

Jake and I stared at each other in shock. So—our date had wandered into a mystery after all, and this time the threat of danger was real. Jake hurried us toward the door but found it locked tight. His key card wouldn't work. "An electronic glitch." He frowned, prying at the handle.

The echo of angry voices sent a chill down my spine. Jake rattled the locked door in vain, his eyes clouding with panic. "This was not how I envisioned our evening going."

"The emergency exit!" I whispered, pointing down the dimly lit corridor. Jake grabbed my hand, pulling me into the shadows as a beam of a flashlight slid past.

We headed toward the glowing exit sign and tried the door. "It's jammed too," he whispered back, his breath warm against my cheek. "We have to hide until they leave."

Jake led us back into the gallery of ancient Egyptian artifacts. The silence was taut, waiting to be pierced by the sounds of the thieves' approach. My heart hammered as we slipped inside a marble encasement, pulling the heavy lid mostly closed to avoid detection.

Pressed close in our confined space, the air seemed to crackle between us. My pulse raced where his arm wrapped around me. Some date, I thought wryly. This was not quite the intimacy I had anticipated tonight. I hoped Jake couldn't feel my pulse racing. Focus, I scolded myself. Escape now, romance later.

The thieves' voices echoed closer again. "The security system should be down for another 30 minutes. Let's find the diamond and get out before the backup generator kicks in."

Jake's eyes widened, catching the implication. What happened to the guards? I stifled a gasp as a thief's flashlight beam came inside our coffin, sliding past us as he went to examine a display of golden amulets. My lungs burned, afraid to even breathe too loudly.

At last, the light and their voices retreated down the corridor. Jake shifted, slowly easing the heavy lid open to peer outside. "The coast is clear," he whispered, helping me climb out of the marble encasement. I nearly wept in relief, unsure how much longer my nerves could bear such tension.

We hurried toward another exit, but Jake froze as voices echoed close by again. He pulled me into an alcove, holding a finger to his lips. I caught a whiff of his cologne, felt the steady beat of his heart, and for a moment, forgot the danger we were in.

"Oh, great, the backup power activated!" A thief growled, slamming the emergency door in anger. "Now, how do we escape without being detected?"

Panic rose in my throat as I looked at Jake in dismay. We were locked in the museum with thieves and for now, no way out.

Jake grasped my hand, his eyes clouding with worry. "There has to be another exit. The security office should have unlocked the door by now unless..." His voice trailed off, not wanting to voice what we both feared—the thieves had done something with the guards on duty.

We crept down the dimly lit hallway, alert for any sounds of the thieves returning. My pulse raced as we turned a corner, and the security office came into view, door flung open. I gasped, panic seizing in my chest at the sight of a guard slumped unconscious in a chair and another on the floor.

Jake hurried to check on them. He pressed his fingers to each guard's neck, leaned close to check for breathing. "They are both alive, pulse steady. Just unconscious," Jake said, relief flooding his face. "We have to get help fast. I wish they didn't mess with the cell service in there."

His eyes scanned the office, landing on a phone. "The alarm and security feeds are down, but the landline may still work."

He grabbed the phone but froze, hearing voices approaching. We scrambled into a supply closet as flashlights slid past. My breath caught until the lights faded away.

Jake dialed 911 in the dark closet, keeping his voice low. "We have an emergency at the Fawnwood Museum. The security system is down, and thieves are attempting to steal valuable artifacts. Two guards are injured. Send help immediately."

He hung up as a thief growled in anger, "The cops will be here any minute. Grab as much loot as you can carry, and let's get out of here."

We stayed hidden until the thieves' voices retreated, then slipped out of the closet. Both guards were rousing. We helped them sit up and got each of them water. Jake told them help was on the way, and they should just stay right there.

We went to see what the thieves may have taken, or what damage they might have done. Adrenaline coursed through me as we approached the Egyptian exhibit, not knowing what we may find and not sure they were gone. To my shock, the sarcophagus we had hidden inside just a short time ago was shattered, fragments littering the floor.

Jake stared at the damage in anger and dismay. "Those monsters. Destroying priceless artifacts without a care for history or culture." His voice shook with emotion. "They need to pay for this. No artifact is worth more than human life, but they must face justice for the damage done here tonight."

His words were cut off by the wail of sirens outside. "Looks like the cavalry has arrived!"

Jake and I headed toward the front doors. Blue and red lights flashed outside as officers emerged, weapons drawn. Jake and I hurried to greet them, relieved the thieves' reign of terror was over. "They're gone. They left through the emergency exit in the Egyptian wing. They might still be close by."

The head officer approached us. "We arrived as soon as we received your call. Are you positive they have left the building?"

"The thieves fled just before you pulled up, though not before causing substantial damage and stealing several smaller artifacts. The door to the Egyptian wing was left open." Jake told the officer. "The two on-duty guards are in the security office. They need medical attention. They are awake now, but they were unconscious when we first found them."

My heart sank at the thought of the treasures lost inside. "You two should come with us to provide statements about what occurred here tonight, and we will need a full inventory of what was taken and destroyed as soon as that can be assessed."

Jake placed a hand on my back, guiding me to follow the officer outside. My legs felt weak with leftover fear and adrenaline.

As we emerged from the museum, a familiar figure caught my eye. Harry, worry etched into his features, hurried over to where we stood.

The sight of him usually filled me with relief and comfort. Not tonight. The tension of our last encounter still hung in the air.

Harry's eyes clouded with pain as he took in the undeniable truth—Jake's hand resting intimately on my back, the eager way I gazed up at him. We were on a date, and Harry had been forced to witness it.

His jaw tightened. "I came as soon as I heard about the break-in." His tone was icy, detached. The awkwardness hung thick in the air between us.

I opened my mouth to say ... what? An apology seemed insufficient. An explanation impossible. Jake and I had crossed a line this evening that couldn't be walked back for anyone's sake.

Harry abruptly turned his eyes away. "If you two will come down to the station to provide official statements..." He stalked off without waiting for a response, eager to escape our presence.

Chapter 15

P olly and I left the apartment and headed for the café, ready to tackle the day's tasks, while the first rays of sunlight painted the sky with a gentle warmth. "Thanks for coming in with me so early," I told her. "Thomas closed up last night, so there is no telling what may have happened."

Polly saluted cheerfully. "Your wish is my command, cap'n! This place will be shipshape in no time."

I unlocked the door, bracing myself for the disaster within. The lingering smell of scorched milk hung in the air. Broken glass and pastries were in the trashcan, and some glass still littered the floor where Thomas had apparently dropped an entire tray. And in the middle of the counter sat our battered espresso machine, a small fire hazard in its own right after Thomas's last attempt at repairs.

Polly let out a low whistle. "Looks like a storm hit and left a mess in its wake. You really ought to make Tommy walk the plank for this nonsense."

I sighed, grabbing a broom. "He means well, just has terrible luck. And even worse hand-eye coordination."

"At this rate, you'll be out of dishes and glasses by the end of the week if something doesn't change."

Polly's quip gave me pause. She was right. Thomas's clumsiness had caused one too many disruptions and almost more in expenses than income. As his friend, I hated to reprimand him, but as his boss, something had to be done.

"You're right," I told Polly. "His heart's in the right place, but we can't continue like this. I'll have a talk with Thomas about sticking to the register and scheduling an extra pair of hands in the kitchen, at least until we replace that deathtrap of an espresso machine."

Polly strode up behind me as she nodded in agreement. "A good plan, cap'n. Now, time to swab the deck!"

As we cleaned, I recounted the events of last night to Polly. "You'll never believe the adventure Jake and I found ourselves in after I met him at the museum." Polly was in bed before I got back home, and after all the excitement, I was too tired to wake her then.

Polly raised an eyebrow, pausing at mopping up spilled milk. "Do tell!"

I launched into the story of hearing the thieves, dashing from one hiding spot to another, including the Egyptian sarcophagus. Being trapped, finding the guards, and finally being able to call the police.

Polly sighed dreamily. "How romantic! Well, aside from the mortal peril bit. I knew that handsome museum guard would sweep you off your feet if you gave him half a chance!"

I blushed at her implication. "It was an interesting first date, if nothing else. At least until Detective Harry showed up."

Polly nearly dropped her mop. "Detective Ex stumbled upon your secret rendezvous? Do tell me there was jealousy and angst and delicious drama!"

I groaned. Trust Polly to be more interested in the romantic entanglements than the near-death experience. "There was definite awkwardness all around. Harry realized Jake and I were on a date and reacted ... coldly, to say the least." The hurt I had seen in Harry's eyes filled me with regret. I sighed, "Just another complication to sort out, as if I needed more drama in my life."

"A juicy love triangle!" Polly cried gleefully. At my exasperated look, she cleared her throat. "I mean, how distressing. Still, what an adventure to share with Jake, at least. Hiding inside an ancient coffin—the story alone is a meet-cute for grandchildren!"

I threw my cleaning rag at her with a laugh. Trust Polly to find the whimsical side of disaster. Her playful teasing lifted my mood, reminding me that despite complications, time spent with Jake had kindled a spark I wasn't ready to extinguish just yet.

"So." Polly leaned on her mop, eyes gleaming with curiosity. "What happens now between you and the charming Jake?"

I sighed, wiping down tables as I collected my thoughts. "I don't know. We didn't exactly have time to talk about it after the thieves left and the police came. And then with Harry coming to the crime scene and heading to the station..." I trailed off. The hurt in Harry's eyes filled me with a pang of regret once more.

Polly waved her hand dismissively. "Detective Ex will come around. The question is, do you want to explore whatever's brewing between you and Jake?"

Did I? The memory of closeness in the cramped darkness, and Jake's arm wrapped securely around me, brought the hint of a smile to my face. "Yes, I rather think I do. If he's willing to brave another outing after last night's chaos, that is."

"From what you've told me, that man would follow you into mortal peril and back again if it meant winning your favor." Polly grinned, eyes dancing. "Running this way and that to avoid thieves on a first date and still eager to see you again - if that's not determination, I don't know what is!"

Her enthusiasm was infectious, lifting away any doubts and replacing them with giddy anticipation. "You're right. When things settle down at the café, I'll give Jake a call. After adventures like we shared, how could we not go on a proper second date?"

Polly raised her coffee in a toast. "That's the spirit! Now then, time to make this place shine before these 'settling down' and 'proper dates' commence!"

After a long and exhausting morning, I sat across from Thomas at a quiet corner of the café, sipping our afternoon coffees. The conversations and laughter of customers provided a comforting background noise as I gathered my thoughts.

"Thomas," I began, deciding honesty was the best approach. "You know I appreciate everything you do for the café, right?"

He looked up, surprise etching his face. "Of course, Lola. Are you going to fire me?"

I took a deep breath and plowed on. "Your ... enthusiasm in the kitchen and with the espresso machine. It's causing some issues."

Thomas blinked, then frowned as he took in my words. "Is this about the mess from last night?" I nodded, my heart going out to him. "But it isn't just last night. So many dishes and cups, and glasses have been broken, and Thomas, you also need to stick to the proper dress code during business hours. Where is your uniform jacket?"

Thomas looked startled, glancing down at his casual shirt. "Oh, sorry, Lola! I spilled coffee on my jacket this morning and sent it to the cleaners. Won't happen again, I promise."

I sighed, hoping this was the last of the day's mishaps. "Thomas, you're a great asset to the café, but perhaps it's time to admit the kitchen may not be your forte. I think it might be better if you stick to the register and customer interactions for a while. We'll also try to get an extra pair of hands in the kitchen until we replace that espresso machine."

Thomas was silent for a moment, his expression unreadable. Then, to my relief, he let out a sigh and nodded. "You're right, Lola. I want what's best for the café, even if it means stepping away from the kitchen. I'm just happy you are not going to fire me. I'll stick to the register and interacting with the customers."

Relief washed over me. "Thank you, Thomas. I'm glad you understand."

Our agreement set in place, we returned to the bustle of the café. With Polly's infectious cheer and Thomas now redirecting his energy where it was most needed, I was hopeful for the first time that day. Little did I know, my heart would soon face a new challenge entirely.

I grabbed my phone during a lull in customers, pulse racing, as I dialed Jake's number. After last night, speaking to him felt both exhilarating and nerve-racking.

He answered on the third ring. "Hello?" His usual playful lilt was missing.

"Jake, it's Lola. I was hoping we could plan another date to make up for last night's being cut short by the big adventure."

There was a pause. "Lola. How's the café today?" His question caught me off guard. I had expected him to enthusiastically suggest when we could meet again, not make casual small talk.

"We've been busy. But I wanted to hear your voice ... see if you were free this evening or tomorrow night?" I cringed at the neediness in my tone.

Another pause. "My schedule's a bit up in the air right now." Jake's noncommittal response twisted my stomach into knots. "There's a lot going on at the museum, you understand?"

The excuses sounded hollow. I swallowed hard against the lump rising in my throat. "Is everything okay?"

"Of course. Just busy." His tone remained cordial but lacking warmth. "We'll figure something out soon. Talk to you later." Before I could voice the confusion and hurt his indifference had sparked, the line disconnected.

I lowered the phone in disbelief, missing his usual affectionate farewell. Last night replayed in my mind; the playful smiles, tender embraces, feeling we could face any challenge together. Now it seemed I had imagined the connection we shared.

Polly strode over, her customary cheer fading at my expression. "What is it, Lola? You look as if you've seen a ghost."

I relayed the stilted conversation, chest tightening. "He's changed, Polly. After everything last night meant, now Jake can scarcely commit to another date?" I bit my lip, hating the desperation in my tone. "Perhaps I'm just being needy ... expecting too much, too soon?"

"Nonsense." Polly squeezed my hand in support. "There's more to this than meets the eye. I'll do some subtle investigating to see if we can figure out what's bothering Jake. In the meantime, keep that pretty chin up!"

Chapter 16

The last customers trickled out for the evening as I began the familiar ritual of closing up the café. Polly left early to catch the sunset for a painting she was working on. With only a couple of customers left, I sent everyone else home. I needed some time to myself, even if it was while also cleaning. My mind wandered to Jake, the memory of his arm snuggly around me in that sarcophagus still vivid and tangible, a stark contrast to the harsh tone in his voice during our earlier call. I longed for a return to that closeness, troubled by secrets—or were they complications?—that seemed bent on tearing us apart as soon as we had met.

A sharp knock at the back door, a staccato beat that echoed through the now-empty café, jarred me from my reverie.

Expecting it to be a late delivery or maybe Jake coming to apologize, I opened it to find an envelope on the step. I looked both ways, but there wasn't anyone in sight. The familiar phrases he'd texted me that day after our exchange on the phone—"sorry," "need to talk," "not what it seems"—seemed ominously foreboding and utterly mysterious.

My name was scrawled in an unfamiliar hand on the envelope. My pulse quickened, drumming a swift rhythm in my ears. I bent down and cautiously picked it up, turning it this way and that, but there were no other markings of any kind. I tore the envelope open, the crisp sound of tearing paper piercing the silence of the café.

Photos fell out, grainy but unmistakable, each snapshot stirring a dreadful realization that Jake might not just be a liar, but a killer too. Jake walking into the museum the night of the masquerade ball, glancing furtively behind him. He told me he was not working that night. The timestamps showed they were taken shortly before the time of Worthington's murder.

My hands trembled, the edges of the photos crinkling under the grip of my fingers. The world seemed to drop out from under me, a cold emptiness spreading from my stomach and prickling across my skin. My stomach churned as I reflected on the words written on a scrap of paper left in the envelope from a mysterious stranger—a warning about trust and deception, about Jake not being who he seemed to be, and alluding to Jake actually being the one that murdered Mr. Worthington.

I was shocked. How had I not recognized the deception concealed behind Jake's tender stare each time I looked into his eyes? The truth now glared at me, terrible in its obviousness—our whirlwind romance had been a masquerade, a dance of deception. Each sweet word, each smoldering glance, was nothing more than a mask, carefully crafted to cast an alluring spell and blind me to who he really was while I poured out my heart to him without reserve.

Hot tears of anger and betrayal burned my eyes. Had I trusted him, defended him, only to become another dupe caught in his web of deceit? Could it be that the Jake I knew and loved had never truly existed—was he a phantom, a sweet dream from which I now awakened to a bitter reality?

There remained a flicker of hope that some logical explanation might emerge to make sense of this madness. A hope that Jake, despite his lies, wasn't capable of something as monstrous as murder. Maybe the stranger was wrong. Maybe there was a reason, a good one. I had to confront him, though the prospect filled me with anguish over ultimate truths I did not wish to face. Grabbing my keys with trembling hands, I headed for the museum before doubts arose to weaken my resolve.

Jake looked up in surprise as I stalked into the security office, fixing him with a piercing gaze through eyes rimmed in red from tears shed in anger and sorrow. "We need to talk. Now!"

He paled at my curt tone, eyes darting to the photos I gripped tightly in my hands. "Where did you get those?"

I stepped forward and threw the photos at him; they fluttered and spun before falling like dying birds onto his desk.

"Never mind where I got them. What I want—no, what I demand—to know is why you felt compelled to lie to me about being at the museum the night that Worthington was murdered!" I spat, my voice trembling with a cocktail of emotions—fear, anger, betrayal. "Are you involved, Jake?"

Once again, tears blurred my vision, their salty sting a harsh reminder of the bitter truth I was facing.

"Lola, I can explain." Jake ran a hand through his hair, looking stricken. "I didn't lie to hurt you. There are ... complications I can't discuss. Please, you have to trust me." He reached for my hand, but I jerked away.

"Trust you?" I scoffed. "It seems you've done nothing but lie all along. How can I believe anything you say now?"

Jake flinched as if I had struck him. "I never meant to deceive you; I swear. My situation is complex, but know that my feelings for you were real." His expression pleaded for understanding. "If there was any way to make you see the truth..."

I remained unmoved, fists clenched at my sides. The words from the note echoed in my mind—'beware the masquerade'. His masquerade. "The time for your masquerade and my blind trust has passed." With an effort, I steadied my voice, my words a mask to hide the pain. "Goodbye, Jake."

As I turned to leave, he reached out to me, "Lola, please. I beg you to listen..."

But I was already out the door, his pleas swallowed by the echoing halls of the museum.

I unlocked our apartment door, heart heavy and eyes still stinging. A flicker of a smile played on my lips as I found Polly, still in her baking apron, dancing around the kitchen to a lively salsa tune. As she saw me, her grin faded, and she immediately switched off the music.

"Lola, darling. What happened?" she asked, her brows furrowing with concern.

I shook my head, struggling to keep the tears at bay. "I'd rather not talk about it right now, Polly. It's just ... it's serious. I need a moment to gather my thoughts."

Polly nodded understandingly and reached out to squeeze my shoulder. "I'll make us some chamomile tea. You go freshen up."

I retreated to the sanctuary of my room, sinking into the bed. The silence of the room amplified the chaos in my mind, the pieces of the evening replaying in an agonizing loop. Jake's face, his pleas, the damning photographs... I stared at the ceiling, forcing slow, deep breaths until the knots in my stomach loosened slightly.

Emerging from my room after a half-hearted attempt to wash away the day, I found Polly had set up a small sanctuary in the living room. The scent of chamomile wafted from two steaming mugs on the coffee table, accompanied by a plate of our favorite vanilla and almond cookies.

Polly, the master of dramatic gestures, unveiled our living room, now transformed into what she affectionately termed the 'heartbreak recovery zone'. "Voila!" she announced with a flourish, "Comfort food and a comfy couch–the only known cure for all of life's problems, including potential boyfriend situations."

We sank into the cushions, sipping the hot, calming tea. Polly waited patiently, her hand a comforting presence on mine. I knew she wouldn't pry, would let me share in my own time.

After a few silent moments, I found my voice. "Jake lied to me, Polly. About where he was the night of the murder. He might... He might be involved." The confession hung in the air, heavy with the weight of my hurt and betrayal. I relayed the evening's events, my voice quivering. By the time I finished, tears pricked at the corners of my eyes.

Polly drew me into a hug, her arms strong and comforting. "Lola, sweetheart, I'm so sorry. But remember, sometimes things aren't what they seem on the surface. Maybe there's more to Jake's story."

"But how can I trust him, Polly? How can I be with someone who might be a murderer?"

Polly's eyes held mine, her brows furrowing as she grappled with the weight of my words. "Lola, that's a serious accusation. And a terrifying thought. But we don't have all the facts, just photos that place him there." She paused, choosing her words carefully. "It doesn't automatically make him guilty. As hard as it is, maybe we need to hold off on judgment until we know more. There might be an explanation. It might not be the one we want, but rushing to conclusions won't help either of you."

Chapter 17

An early somber breakfast was followed by Polly encouraging me to take a walk, to try to clear my head. After the confrontation, I needed time to think. I needed to piece together the events and understand what I was missing.

Walking the familiar streets did nothing to suppress the storm in my mind, but a glimpse of memory suddenly emerged. It was the night of the masquerade ball. I found that dagger under one of the cabinets, Jake said he thought it was from a collection that was stolen years ago. It had blood on it, but he had asked me to hide it, saying, 'Lola, this is important. I need you to keep this safe. It could prove my innocence one day.'

Remembering Jake's desperate eyes sent a chill down my spine. That dagger. I had hidden it under the floorboards of the café. It suddenly clicked; Jake was being framed, and the dagger could prove his innocence.

I started running, not caring about the bemused looks of the few other pedestrians around. I needed to get to the café. I needed to find that dagger.

The café was a welcome sight, standing stoically in the early morning light. Unlocking the door, I rushed in, the silent empty tables bearing mute witness to my urgency. Underneath a floorboard behind the counter, hidden from prying eyes, was the loose floorboard, the secret makeshift vault I had consigned Jake's dagger to.

Kneeling, I pried it up, my heart pounding in my chest.

I felt a twinge of hope as I reached into the compartment, but my heart sank when I found it empty. No dagger. It was gone.

A wave of desperation washed over me. I ransacked the area, hoping that it had merely slipped out of the hiding spot. But it was nowhere to be found. The only piece of evidence that Jake said might prove him innocent one day ... had vanished.

I slumped to the floor, leaning against the counter, my mind racing with possibilities. How had this happened? Who else knew about this hiding place, and the dagger?

And then I heard the door jiggle and the jingle of keys. My heart stopped. I quickly pushed the floorboard back into place and stood up just as the door creaked open. In walked Thomas, who was known more for his clumsiness than his punctuality, was surprisingly early.

Then again, so was I.

"Lola? What are you doing here so early?" He looked surprised but also a bit pleased with himself. "I thought I would be the first one in today. Trying to make up for everything. After our talk the other day, I realized I'd better put in more of an effort before I really do get fired."

His words hung in the air as I quickly tried to think of an explanation. "Just ... checking for a ... mice problem," I finally said, pointing vaguely at the floor. I inwardly cringed at my poor excuse, but Thomas merely shrugged, accepting the explanation as he moved behind the counter to start the coffee machine.

"Mice, huh?" Thomas echoed, quirking an eyebrow as he laughed at my sudden pest control duty. I chuckled along too, hoping it would mask the rush of panic that surged beneath my façade.

"You're a woman of many talents, Lola." I forced a smile in return, but my panic rose as I saw that the floorboard hiding the secret vault was still askew.

As he filled the water in the machine, Thomas started talking about his past, sharing stories of his clumsy adventures and missteps. His self-deprecating tales painted a picture starkly at odds with the resolute man before me now. Regret tinged his words, along with a steely determination.

"I've stumbled through more jobs than I can count." He snorted, shaking out the coffee filter with a bit more vigor than necessary. "Some bosses just love seeing you fall on your face, you know? One used to relish rehashing every little mistake." His knuckles whitened around the metal edge of the filter basket. "Pointing out every silly flaw."

When he glanced up, his eyes held a distant glint, as if seeing something—or someone—from long ago.

"But this place is home." He set the filled basket onto the machine with a metallic thud. "But I know, another slipup and I'm out. So here I am, bright and early. Time for a change, don't you think?"

With a flick of the switch, the coffee maker hummed to life. Thomas disappeared into the kitchen, leaving me alone with my pounding heart and damning knowledge. The floorboard gaped up at me, a conspicuous reminder of the secret beneath.

The image of the empty hiding spot played in my mind like a broken record, accompanied by a desperate question—what if the dagger was still there? My hand itched to lift the floorboard again, to dive deeper into the unknown.

But just as I was about to succumb to my curiosity, Thomas's cheery humming resonated from the kitchen. The familiar sound jolted me back to reality. The stakes were too high to risk discovery now.

The kitchen door creaked ominously, signaling his impending return. I quickly shoved the floorboard down and put my foot on it. It was a desperate attempt, a Band-Aid solution, but all I could do at the moment.

The door swung open, revealing a beaming Thomas with two steaming mugs of coffee. Oblivious to the turmoil within me, he handed me one of the mugs, a smile lighting up his face. I mirrored his smile with all the strength I could muster, aware of the secret lying just beneath my foot.

Thomas busied himself preparing the café for opening while chatting cheerily with the few early customers trickling in. I hovered by the counter, clutching my coffee mug, torn between wanting to continue my secret search and maintaining an air of normalcy.

Just then, the bell above the door rang as Miss Pepper bustled in. "Good morning, Thomas, dear!" she exclaimed. "The usual for me, extra cream, two sugars."

"Coming right up, Miss Pepper," Thomas replied, turning to prepare her coffee with his usual clumsy enthusiasm. His elbow bumped a precariously balanced tray of mugs, sending them tumbling to the floor with a crash.

Miss Pepper gasped. "Oh, Thomas, you silly boy, you've gone and broken my favorite mug!"

Thomas stammered an apology, his cheeks flushing in embarrassment as he scrambled to clean up the mess. In his haste, he knocked over the creamer, splashing the white liquid across the counter.

I bit my lip, torn between amusement and sympathy at Thomas's plight. His determination to do better was admirable, but his natural clumsiness continued to prevail.

With the chaos and chatter in the café, I realized this could be an opportunity to lift the floorboard undetected again. I kneeled down, pulling up the uneven edge of the wood. To my surprise, there, wedged deeper in the crevice, was a glint of metal. I felt a surge of hope—could it be the dagger?

Just then, Miss Pepper's voice rose above the chaos. "Thomas, the creamer is empty! How will I have my coffee without cream?"

Thomas yelped in dismay, rushing to fetch more cream from the kitchen. In his hasty return trying to go around the counter to put the creamer down for Miss Pepper, he slipped on the still-wet floor, tumbling forward with the containers in hand. A flood of white liquid gushed across the counter, pouring over the edge and onto my back as I kneeled by the counter.

I gasped as I stood, soaked in cream, to find Thomas peering over the counter, his eyes widening in horror at the sight of me. "Lola! Oh no, I'm so sorry!" he cried.

The entire café fell silent, all eyes turning to the spectacle of Thomas's catastrophic clumsiness. I caught Thomas's eyes, then burst into laughter at the absurdity of the situation, the tension and panic of the past hour releasing in a fit of giggles.

Thomas began laughing too, a deep belly laugh joining in with the lighter sound of my own. The other customers chuckled as I grabbed a towel, drenched but still grinning.

"Well, I did want an extra splash of cream in my coffee," I quipped, eliciting another round of laughter from the crowd.

Miss Pepper clicked her tongue in amusement. "Oh, you dears, whatever am I to do with the two of you?"

Thomas gave me an apologetic smile as he rushed to bring me more towels and to clean the spill.

The laughter slowly faded as the customers returned to their own conversations, the bustle and chatter dying down. Thomas's smile wavered as the realization hit him that his clumsiness may have cost him his job. His eyes held a glimmer of panic and regret.

I felt a pang of guilt, remembering how Thomas had shared his resolve to do better here to avoid losing this place he called home. I bit my lip, moving closer to give his arm a reassuring squeeze.

"Don't worry, I'll have a word with the manager," I joked softly. "It was just an accident. She can't let you go over a few broken mugs. But I have a feeling she may need to doc your pay after all of this. Register and customer interaction, remember?"

Thomas sighed, his shoulders sagging in relief. "Thanks, Lola. I understand. I don't know why I'm so prone to these foolish mistakes. I just wanted to show I could handle the responsibility, and here I've gone and made another mess of things."

"You do just fine most days," I replied gently. "No one expects you to be perfect. And your heart is in the right place, even if your elbows aren't."

Thomas laughed at that, his smile returning at my teasing reassurance. I was glad to see his spirits brighten again. His openness made me feel I could share in return.

"Thomas, I should confess ... there weren't really any mice," I began hesitantly. He looked puzzled until understanding dawned in his eyes.

"You were looking for something under the floorboards, weren't you?" he asked. I nodded, feeling a weight lift off my shoulders as I divulged at least part of the secret I had been keeping. Thomas grew serious, his voice dropping to a conspiratorial whisper.

"Lola, if there's anything I can do to help, or anything you need to tell me, I'm here. I may be clumsy, but I can keep a secret, and I care about what happens to you and Polly and this place."

I gave him a grateful smile, touched by his heartfelt offer. There were still parts of the mystery I needed to keep concealed, but maybe Thomas could actually be more help than I'd thought. "Thank you, Thomas. I may take you up on that soon. For now, though, how about I help you pick up these broken pieces?"

Chapter 18

"You told THOMAS WHAT?" Polly's tone escalated in disbelief, her grip on the steering wheel tightening as we maneuvered through the town towards the veterinary clinic. The air was thick with tension, a far cry from the usual jovial banter accompanying our drives. I had confided in Thomas about hiding the dagger under the café floorboards and had not consulted Polly about the decision. What made matters more complicated was Thomas's offer to help, requiring me to reveal this clandestine decision.

A gust of air blew from the car's vents, doing little to cool the heat of Polly's disbelief. She shook her head as she processed my revelation. "Lola, what were you thinking?" Her eyes flickered towards me briefly before refocusing on the road, concern etched into the furrows of her brow. "That dagger could be evidence! It's bad enough you took it and hid it just because Jake asked you to. If someone else finds you have it and it is the murder weapon, you and I will be in jail..."

"I know, I know," I sighed, sinking into the cushion of the passenger seat, my fingers worrying the edge of my cardigan. I could still feel the phantom chill of the dagger against my skin. "It seemed like a good decision at the moment. But now everything's become such a mess." I watched the scenery pass by, the shops and trees blending into a blur of color, mirroring my muddled thoughts.

The stern line of Polly's mouth softened, and she glanced at me, her hand leaving the steering wheel for a moment to give my arm a comforting pat. "You were only trying to help Jake." Her voice was softer now, the reproach replaced with understanding. "But from now on, no more secrets between us, and don't tell anyone else about the hiding spot, promise?" Her green eyes met mine, sincerity shining from their depths.

Her simple gesture, combined with her reassuring words, untied the knot of tension in my chest. I turned to her, my lips curving into a small smile, and gave her hand an appreciative squeeze. "Promise, Polly. No more secrets."

My anxiety returned as we entered the vet's office. The sterile smell of the office had me picturing our last visit here - a rerun I hadn't asked for: Dr. Mendel's unexpected find that had triggered a biopsy and a harrowing wait to determine if it was cancerous or indicative of another dangerous condition. The waiting period had been interminable, each day fraught with worry.

Dr. Mendel, with his white coat and kindly face, welcomed us with an assuring smile that seemed to lighten the room. "Ladies, I have good news," he announced, leading us into the familiar exam room. Tetley, our dear companion, was snuggled down in his carrier. "The biopsy results have come in. The mass is benign. Tetley is perfectly healthy otherwise. I want to check the lump again to see if it has grown or changed any. Right now, we can just leave it alone, but if it grows, we may need to remove it for Tetley's comfort."

Relief rushed in like a tidal wave, and my legs turned to jelly. The examination table became my impromptu crutch. Polly's face broke into a grin that mirrored my own relief, and she thanked Dr. Mendel with a fervor that made him chuckle.

Fumbling with the latch, I freed Tetley from his carrier and lifted him into my arms, holding him close to me. His fur was warm and comforting, and as I buried my face into his softness, I felt a bubble of joy swell within me. Tetley seemed to sense my elation, nuzzling into my neck, cooing contentedly.

Polly moved to us then, her laughter ringing out in the sterile room as she threw her arms around both Tetley and me. "Thank goodness!" The relief in her voice echoed my own sentiments. We had imagined every possible scenario, most of them filled with dread and sorrow.

I placed Tetley on the examination table so Dr. Mendel could check the lump. As Tetley received his clean bill of health, the tension ebbed from my shoulders, leaving behind a soothing calm.

Polly and I were about to depart when a hunched figure in the waiting area yanked my gaze. There was Jake, his hand rhythmically stroking a shaggy terrier, whose listlessness tugged at my heartstrings.

His eyes darted up to meet mine, as hesitant as a jaywalker on a freeway. A bitter taste rose at the back of my tongue, a ghost of our encounters, my confrontation, and the confusion they left.

The little dog let out a whine that could have been a siren for all its urgency, his little body trembling like a leaf in a storm. Jake's hand slowed, fingers pressing comfort into the dog's fur. The furrowed lines on his forehead deepened as if he was silently communicating with the terrier.

Feeling Polly's light touch on my arm, I turned to see her nodding towards Jake. "We should see if we can lend a hand," she suggested, her words whisking away any lingering hesitations like a broom to cobwebs. Taking a steadying breath, I nodded in agreement and moved towards Jake, aiming for a reassuring smile.

"Hello, Jake. I didn't even know you had a dog." My voice was softer, laced with sympathy. "I'm sorry to see your furry friend under the weather. What's his name?" Jake's eyes met mine again, surprise replacing the earlier hesitance as his tension seemed to slacken.

"Thank you, Lola. This is Bubbles." His voice was hushed, matching the subdued ambiance. "He's been unwell for a few days. I fear it's something grave." His hand never stopped its rhythmic petting, lulling the dog's shivers into a grudging calm. As I watched, bits of my irritation and confusion crumbled away like a stale cookie, revealing the man with a heart of gold I once knew.

"I bet the vet will have your buddy bouncing back in no time, Jake. He's too cute to be under the weather for long!" I said, reaching out to give the terrier a gentle scratch behind the ears. The terrier's tail gave a faint, tentative wag. A small, grateful smile lifted the corners of Jake's lips.

"I hope so too. Thanks, Lola." His eyes clung to mine, gratitude brewing in those depths like a comforting cup of tea.

Polly, seizing an opportunity, chimed in then, her voice filled with the same easy camaraderie she usually saved for our afternoons at the café. "Jake, how about a little company while you wait? We can take turns petting this little fellow. I bet he'd like that."

Jake seemed to hesitate, glancing at his terrier, then back to us. But finally, a small nod. "I think he'd like that. Thanks, Lola, Polly."

As the tension eased with our settling into the wait, Polly's phone buzzed from her pocket, cutting through the low hum of the veterinary office. She glanced at the caller ID, her eyebrows knitting together. "It's the café. The coffee machine is on the fritz again." She cast a conspiratorial glance my way, a hint of mischief playing at the corners of her mouth. Despite the tension, my face creased up into a smile. Polly had a knack for dramatic exits.

"Go on," I said, nudging her gently, my eyes involuntarily sliding back to Jake. "We'll be fine."

With a thankful nod, she quickly exited the room, leaving Jake and me alone. An awkward silence followed, punctuated only by the soft, pitiful whines of his sick terrier. A mild tension hung in the air, but I shook it off, reaching out to give the little dog a comforting pet.

"He hasn't been eating well, has he?" I asked, hoping to keep the conversation light, focused on the pup.

Jake's sigh carried an echo of his worry. "Not for the past few days. I'm just hoping it's not as bad as it looks."

We continued to chat about the terrier, his symptoms, possible causes, our past disagreements melting into the background as shared concern took center stage. Seeing this as an opportunity, I decided to talk to him about the dagger and tell him where it was.

"Jake, I need to tell you something," I began, my voice firm despite the nerves. He looked at me, surprise briefly flickering across his face before he composed himself. "It's about the dagger..."

A look of adorable confusion scrunched up his forehead, but he stayed quiet, letting me continue. "I hid the dagger ... under some loose floorboards in the café behind the counter."

The surprise was evident on his face. "The dagger? The one I asked you to hide?"

I nodded, feeling the knot in my stomach tighten. "Yes, the one from the museum. It seemed like the safest place at the time, but now

I realize that this whole situation is far more complicated than I'd initially thought. Everything's become ... messy."

Jake was silent for a moment, his expression unreadable. Then he took a deep breath and nodded. "Lola, thank you for keeping it safe. I know it's put you in an uneasy position."

His words did nothing to assuage my anxiety. "Jake, I need to know more about this dagger. Is there something you haven't told me? Because as things stand, it feels like you're either being framed or ... or..." I couldn't finish the sentence, but I didn't have to. The accusation hung in the air, as tangible as the tension.

Jake met my eyes, the usual twinkle in his eye replaced with a serious glint. "I understand your doubts, Lola. I'm as baffled by this situation as you are. But one thing I can assure you of is that I am innocent. And I think this dagger just might be my get-out-of-jail-free card."

"Jake, what is this really about?" I asked. Before he could answer, his phone rang, jolting us both. The color drained from his face as he looked at the caller ID. "It's the museum," he muttered, answering the call. A moment later, he dropped the phone, his face turning ashen. "Brittany DuPont is dead."

Chapter 19

"Oh, great," Polly exclaimed as she slammed down the morning newspaper onto the counter of our cozy Gallery Café. Her disheveled hair framed her wide-eyed face, a look of disbelief was etched onto her features. "Now, it seems we've got a serial killer on the loose." Polly rolled her eyes dramatically. "Honestly, what's next? Are we going to find out the mayor is a secret werewolf?"

The café was humming with its usual early morning cacophony—coffee machines whirring, the clink of cutlery, and hushed conversations underlined by the subtle soundtrack of a vintage jazz record. The breakfast crowd was oblivious to the undercurrent of unease; their world revolved around frothy lattes and freshly prepared avocado toast.

As the morning light streamed through the window, the colorful chalkboard menu came to life—steaming cups and smiling pastries, all drawn by Polly's artistic hand, waltzed on the wall, a vivid display of her boundless creativity and passion that infused every corner of her world.

I looked up from the cash register, raising an eyebrow. "Polly, don't exaggerate," I started to say, but the grim look on her face stopped me. I wiped my hands on my apron and walked over, picking up the paper. The paper felt slightly damp from the morning dew, and the ink left a faint smudge on my fingertips as I eagerly scanned the text.

The headline screamed at me, confirming Polly's statement: "Brittany DuPont, Prominent Museum Curator And Art Collector, Found Dead—Second Death in Connection to Museum?"

A chill ran down my spine. Just yesterday, Jake had told me the same, his face ashen and voice trembling. Brittany DuPont was the next victim. As I scanned the article, my mind started racing. Two murders, both connected to the museum, and all signs seemed to point at Jake. But if Jake wasn't the killer, who was? And more importantly, who would be next? The reality of the situation hit me; our quaint little town was no longer the idyllic haven it once was. At least, not right now.

The day wore on, but the heaviness in the air lingered. Our regular customers sensed the tension, their customary banter replaced with hushed whispers and furtive glances around the café. Polly and I exchanged worried looks, wondering how much longer we could maintain the façade of normalcy. "Well, on the bright side," I quipped, attempting to lighten the mood, "at least the serial killer hasn't developed a taste for avocado toast ... yet."

As the lunch rush subsided, Jake burst through the door, his face flushed and his eyes wild. "I think I've found something!" he announced, not bothering to lower his voice. I noticed how the afternoon light accentuated the sharp lines of Jake's jaw and the captivating glint in his eyes, making it harder for me to focus on the dire news at hand.

Polly and I exchanged glances before quickly ushering him into the back room, away from prying ears.

Once we were safely out of earshot, Jake continued, breathless, "I was going through Brittany's office at the museum, trying to find any clues that might lead to who might want her dead. I found this." He pulled out a crumpled piece of paper, covered in hastily scribbled notes and what looked like a rough sketch of an artifact. "It's a list of artifacts that were supposed to be part of the museum's new exhibit, but there's one piece that's been crossed out. I think it might be the missing link."

Polly squinted at the paper, her brow furrowed. "But what does this have to do with the murders?"

Jake sighed, his eyes darkening. "Brittany was threatening to expose the truth about some of the artifacts in the museum's collection, just like Worthington before her. They believed some were forgeries meant to increase their value and the museum's prestige. This list must be what got Worthington killed first, and now Brittany."

Polly's eyes widened. "So you think your cousin Victor, or someone at the museum, killed them both to keep these secrets hidden?"

Jake nodded grimly. "It has to be Victor," he replied darkly. "As the curator, he has been amassing secret treasures for himself for years. Remember, spying on him hiding valuable artifacts away rather than displaying them properly. Worthington and his lover Brittany were going to reveal the truth, so they were both silenced. I always suspected the museum's board of directors were more concerned with appearances than integrity."

My mind raced as I tried to process this new revelation. Victor had always given me the creeps with his keen interest and the way he barked orders at the museum staff. And we had caught him hiding artifacts before rather than displaying them as a curator should. "But why would Victor or the board go to such extreme lengths? Double murder seems rather excessive just to protect the museum's reputation."

"You'd be surprised how far some will go to preserve power and status," Jake replied darkly. "I fear Brittany may not be the last victim if we don't find solid evidence to expose the truth and catch the killer."

All this time Brittany had been working to reveal the truth, while danger lurked unseen. Guilt swelled within me that we hadn't been able to protect her. What other lives were at risk if we didn't act quickly?

A chill ran down my spine at Jake's ominous words. The museum had been a pillar of our community, but now its façade crumbled away to reveal the rot underneath. I glanced at the list in Jake's hands, my eyes drawn to the crossed-out artifact. "What can you tell us about this missing artifact?"

Jake glanced at the paper, hesitating. "Honestly, not much. Brittany didn't include any details, likely to protect the information. But since it's the only item crossed out, it must be important."

Polly shook her head, her short blonde pixie hair dancing with the movement. "Art, like life, can be chaotic and unpredictable. I guess that's what makes it so fascinating and terrifying at the same time."

I gulped. "We need to visit Victor again. Ask him a few more questions."

Jake nodded. "Tomorrow. I'll sneak you in the side gate at seven a.m. That's when Victor is due in for an emergency board meeting. I think it might be worth it to spy on that meeting."

The rustling of leaves and the soft chirping of crickets provided a soothing backdrop to our conversation as we strolled through Fawnwood Park, the once welcoming shadows now hiding unknown dangers.

Polly glanced around, hugging her arms tight, then turned to me, a conspiratorial glint in her eye. "Don't you find it odd how Jake always conveniently has clues about these murders?"

I paused. Our charming museum guard had seemed intent on helping us crack this case, but he did have a knack for popping up at just the right moment with another puzzle piece. "He works there after all," I tried to defend him, meekly. "That's how he knows all this stuff..."

Polly shook her head. "Lola, he's a security guard. What other security guard has this sort of unfettered access to private offices and confidential files?"

She had a point. But I tried to downplay it. "He is a DuPont, remember? There's murder in the air. We're all a little on edge. Maybe we're being overly suspicious."

Polly sighed dramatically. "You're right. At this point, I suspect the popcorn vendor has secrets. Nothing in this town is as quaint as it seems anymore!"

I laughed at her theatrics. "Next you'll be telling me old Mrs. Finnegan is running an underground smuggling ring from her bakery."

A snap of a twig sent us darting behind the nearest oak tree, hearts racing until we realized it was just a squirrel. We emerged from our hiding spot in a fit of giggles at our own foolishness.

By the time we came full circle back to the park gates, full darkness had descended. We hurried down the lamp-lit street toward the café, breaths escaping in puffs of white. The familiar shops and homes seemed to hide their own little mysteries, but those secrets would have to wait for the light of day.

As we walked, I couldn't help but notice old Mrs. Thompson peering at us from behind her curtains. She was notorious for being the neighborhood's unofficial news reporter, and I could only imagine the headlines she'd create just from our walk in the park.

Polly glanced over her shoulder, eyes gleaming. "After a day like today, I could use a slice of Mrs. Finnegan's chocolate pecan pie. Race you to the café?"

Chapter 20

The horrible hour of seven a.m. found us skulking into the museum's side entrance, stifling yawns and clutching Styrofoam cups of coffee. Jake—dressed in civilian clothes—flashed us a conspiratorial grin and gestured for quiet, not that Polly needed any encouragement in sneaking around. She was vibrating with glee at our clandestine meeting. I wished I shared her enthusiasm for sleuthing at such an uncivilized time of morning.

Polly stifled an excited giggle, clutching my arm. Sneaking around always gave her a thrill, while I felt a nervous knot in my stomach.

Victor and his cronies were early risers, and whatever schemes they were hatching behind those oak-paneled doors seemed sure to ruin my caffeine buzz.

"Shh, the coast is clear," Jake whispered, peering down the dimly lit hall. His eyes glinted with mischief. We crept behind him, our footsteps echoing too loudly on the marble floors for my liking. There were too many unknowns lurking in the shadows of this old building, and secrets seemed to seep from every crack.

Polly glanced at the gilded frames lining the walls, each holding a stern face staring back at us. "If these old geezers could talk, the stories they'd tell!" she whispered.

"Less talking, more sneaking!" Jake replied, peering around a corner before waving us on frantically.

The boardroom was just ahead, a sliver of light visible underneath the heavy door. As we inched closer, muffled discussion and disagreement could be heard from within. Jake signaled us to stop as footsteps approached from an adjacent room. We shrank into an alcove, barely breathing, as Victor strode by with a troubled scowl.

What secrets hid behind that expression? Did he suspect the truth was closing in? My pulse raced thinking this could be the dangerous man who ended two lives to protect his sinister agenda.

As we hid, I noticed the massive marble statue Victor had been directing the attendants to move previously. A flicker of annoyance crossed Victor's face as he suddenly stopped and turned around. Had he heard us?

My heart leaped into my throat. Jake shoved us unceremoniously into a storage closet, slamming the door just as Victor walked back and peered around the corner, eyes narrowing in suspicion.

We held our breath in the pressing darkness, listening as Victor's footsteps slowly continued down the hall, the audible click of a door signaling he had entered the boardroom.

Polly let out a sigh of relief. "That was close!" she whispered. "Now, how do we spy on them without Victor interrupting us again?"

Jake reached up, pulling on a frayed cord to turn on the single bulb. An impish grin spread across his face as he moved a stack of boxes aside to reveal a worn tapestry on the wall ... and a small hole behind it.

"Through here," he whispered, putting his eye up to the hole. "It seems this storage closet shares a wall with the boardroom. We can see and hear everything through this little mouse hole!"

Polly's eyes gleamed with delight at this revelation. My stomach did another flip—what secrets would we discover, peering into that inner sanctum? I steeled my nerves, taking a turn to peer through the hole. The board members were taking their seats, and it seemed the meeting was just getting started.

We crowded around the little hole in the wall, jostling for a view of the secret proceedings within. My coffee was cold and forgotten, my curiosity overcoming any remaining fatigue.

The board members were an assortment of balding men in varying stages of alertness, clutching leather briefcases and steaming mugs as they took their seats. At the head of the long oak table, Victor shuffled papers with an air of self-importance, eyeing the clock impatiently.

"This emergency meeting will come to order," he proclaimed in a nasal tone. "We have matters of a delicate nature to discuss, so I must remind you that secrecy is of the utmost importance."

A portly man with a bushy mustache spoke up. "Is this about the missing artifact? DuPont's list?"

Missing artifact? DuPont's list must be what Jake found in Brittany's office. I made a mental note to ask him for further details after this escapade was over.

Victor's eyes narrowed. "Your careless tongue will be your downfall, Mr. Barclay. Now, if there are no further breaches of discretion..." He glared around the table, daring anyone to interrupt again. "As you know, certain ... financial discrepancies ... have come to light during a recent audit. Serious allegations which could destroy the reputation of this institution, I'm afraid."

Polly's gasp echoed my own. Jake threw us a worried glance, signaling for continued silence. What sort of shady dealings had Victor embroiled the museum in? His ominous words filled me with dread, and a sense of being in over our heads. Still, there was no turning back now...

A sudden commotion outside made us jump. The double doors to the boardroom flew open with a bang as Marcella DuPont swept into the room, pausing for dramatic effect.

Not a hair was out of place, diamond earrings glinting as she angled her head. But underneath her polished exterior, a cunning gleam in her eye betrayed barely suppressed rage. Marcella was a vision of poise—and pure venom.

The board members seemed to shrink under her scrutiny, years of influence and secrets passing silently between them. Only Victor held her stare, knuckles white around his gavel.

After an agonizing pause, she spoke, each word clipped and measured. "You vile, loathsome creatures. Did you think your webs of deceit would remain unplucked?"

Victor scoffed, though unable to hide a nervous tremor in his voice. "Whatever do you mean, Ms. DuPont? We were conducting private business..."

"Don't insult me with your lies!" Marcella snapped. "My sweet Brittany knew your sins and paid the price for them. Did you truly believe I would not unearth what you so crudely attempted to bury?"

She circled the table slowly, tracing a finger along the oak as if imagining where their necks might soon lie upon it. The board members shrank under her menacing glare, years of shared secrets passing between them.

Only Victor held her stare, knuckles white around the gavel. As she passed behind his chair, he suddenly rose and spun to face her, eyes blazing.

"That's enough of your games, Marcella! We know the truth—you were behind Brittany's death, not I!"

Marcella halted, composure slipping for a brief moment before her mask of haughty indifference slid back into place. "Have you gone mad, Victor? The lies you spew will not save you now."

"Lies, you say?" Victor sneered, tapping a thick folder in front of him. "The proof is here in black and white. Brittany discovered your embezzlement, threatened to turn you in to the authorities. You couldn't risk your lavish kingdom crumbling, so you silenced her forever!"

Marcella's lips curled in contempt. "You fabricated these so-called proofs to save your own skin. My sins are naught compared to the depths you sank to in order to protect your power!"

Victor clenched his fists, pale with rage. Through clenched teeth, he said, "Your sins were always your greed, your thirst for control over all. Even murdering your own blood to keep anyone from daring to take your crown!"

At this accusation, Marcella's composure fell away, diamond-sharp edges glinting from beneath her crumbling façade. With a huff of indignation, she lunged towards Victor, reaching for the folder as she chastised him sharply. "You have no idea what you are talking about!"

A flurry of activity filled the boardroom as the men clearly moved their seats back, ready to jump, surprised gasps echoing around the room. But their movement seemed distant, my vision narrowing to the two figures locked in a struggle for dominance —

Victor had declared a checkmate at last. But in revealing Marcella as the true puppet master, he ensured this twisted game could only end with one of them left standing. However, the real question was how we would make it through this crazy situation to spill the beans on their schemes.

Jake grabbed my arm, eyes wide. "Time to make our not-so-grand exit!"

We hurried down the dim hallway, our bumbling escape hampered by Polly stopping every few feet to snap photos of the priceless art on the walls. "But this is a lost masterpiece!" she protested as Jake tugged her along impatiently.

At the side exit, Jake shoved with all his might, but the door refused to budge. "Must be rusted shut," he muttered. "Of course. Why would anything be easy?"

Raised voices echoed down the hall, getting louder and then going silent. I resisted the urge to bury my face in my hands. "Option two?"

Jake grimaced. "There is no other exit on this side except one that is closer to the front, and we would have to go past the board room again. We can't go out the front door either." He looked around the area, finally grabbing a massive candelabra to use as a battering ram. After several swings, the stubborn lock finally gave way. "Hurry!" said Jake as he pushed us through the door.

No sooner had we stumbled into the crisp morning air than two other security guards came into view, mid-patrol. "Hey, you there! Museum's not open yet..."

Polly and I exchanged a panicked look before bolting across the lawn, slipping and sliding on the wet grass with the befuddled guards shouting at our heels. Stumbling through an elaborately sculpted hedge, we emerged disheveled and leafy haired before a grand fountain. And there, calmly sipping her morning tea as if nothing was amiss, sat Marcella DuPont.

She raised a single eyebrow, amusement glinting in her eyes. "Leaving so soon? The excitement is just beginning inside." Marcella lifted her teacup in a toast, her smug smile following us as we made our getaway from the museum grounds.

Chapter 21

T he rolling hills of Fawnwood Park were alive with laughter under the afternoon sun. As I handed out to-go boxes of Turkish coffee and honeyed baklava from the Gallery Café, our usual banter soon turned to the morning's chilling events.

"After seeing Victor in action, I'm telling you he's off his rocker!" Polly exclaimed through a mouthful of flaky pastry. As always, powdered sugar decorated her freckled nose, clashing with her usual attire of paint-splattered overalls.

I raised an eyebrow, tucking a stray curl behind my ear. "Says the woman who nearly got us caught to photograph a 'lost masterpiece.' That boardroom was no studio, Pol!"

"Ladies, please!" Jake interrupted, running a hand through his artfully tousled hair. He'd had to drop by his apartment to change before his actual shift started in an hour. No one should look that attractive in a museum security uniform. "We were all a bit reckless this morning. But at least we escaped to caffeinate and regroup, right? Nothing like a potential arrest to work up a thirst!" He flashed that heart-stopping grin, diffusing my annoyance. Although, at the back of my mind, there was still the worry that Marcella had called the cops after seeing us sneaking out the side door.

Polly sighed dreamily, then caught herself, cheeks flushing as pink as the baklava. "Ahem, yes, thank you for talking sense into us, Mr. Marple. Where were we?"

"Debating Marcella and Victor's degrees of sinister guilt," I replied, passing around tiny cups of fragrant coffee. "After her performance this morning, I don't buy Marcella's innocent act. She's too calculating by half."

Jake nodded thoughtfully. "I have to agree. Victor may have secrets, but Marcella seems the manipulator here."

Polly groaned, dropping back onto the grass. "Must you both be so sensible? Where's the fun in a logical mystery?" But her eyes gleamed with curiosity at this new line of reasoning.

Jake laughed. "But seriously—let's go over the evidence again."

"Well," I began, taking a sip of the strong coffee. "Let's start with Marcella. We caught her prowling around the museum after hours, right? And she was rummaging through Victor's office, no less."

Jake nodded, adding, "And she was quick to point fingers at Brittany. Almost like she was trying to divert suspicion."

Polly jumped in, "Don't forget the barn! She threatened us. Who even chases people with an SUV?"

Jake winced, rubbing the back of his neck. "Yeah, that story was intense. And if she was in his will or promised money if he died, Worthington's death would secure her finances. She does like her luxuries."

I shot him a dry look. "Understatement of the year, Jake."

Laughter bubbled up between us before I sobered, turning the conversation to Victor. "Victor isn't innocent either. He's been hiding valuable artifacts and acting oddly."

Polly chimed in, "Yeah, and he was furious about Worthington selling the museum land. Remember that argument? He even threatened to resign."

Jake, who had been quiet, finally spoke, "That's not all, remember those plane tickets for the day after the murder? Where was he planning to go?"

I added, "And let's not forget his accusing Marcella at the meeting, hinting that she murdered Brittany to keep her luxurious lifestyle intact. That seemed ... calculated."

Polly sighed heavily, "So, we're back at square one. Either of them could have done it. Are we any closer to finding out who killed Worthington?"

I grinned, settling beside her. "Maybe not just yet. But we deserve to celebrate—we've just narrowed the playing field!"

"To the black widow herself," Jake proclaimed, raising his tiny cup.

"To justice for Brittany!" Polly chimed in. We clinked cups with a giggle, spirits rising.

Polly sighed, checking her watch. "As much as I'd love to continue sleuthing, I have an art class starting in thirty minutes. Duty calls!" She sprung up, brushing grass from her overalls.

"Thanks for the snack, Lola. See you lovebirds later!" She winked, hurrying off across the lawn before I could respond.

An awkward silence fell between Jake and me with Polly's departure. So much had happened since our one odd date, and now everything felt jumbled in my mind.

Jake ran a hand through his hair, glancing at me uncertainly. "I feel like things have been rather ... complicated since the other night. What with all the chaos lately, I wasn't sure if you still..."

I tucked a loose curl behind my ear, pulse racing. In my nervousness, the first question that came to mind was "How is Bubbles doing after his visit to the vet?" I asked.

Jake looked startled but relieved at the change of subject. "Bubbles? Oh, he's doing much better. Thanks for asking. Just had an upset tummy, nothing serious. Spoiled thing probably ate something he shouldn't."

Our lighthearted exchange about Bubbles's mischief eased the tension, but uncertainty lingered about where we stood. I glanced at Jake, pulse racing. His playful smile faded as our eyes met, sobering us both. We couldn't avoid the awkwardness forever. "So, you were asking ... if I still wanted to continue where we left off?" I offered with a nervous chuckle. His eyes lit up briefly, then clouded again.

"Do you?" Jake asked, vulnerability flickering across his features. "I understand if, after everything that's happened, dinner and romance are the last things on your mind. We certainly seemed to stumble upon more intrigue and danger than most couples on a first date!"

I sighed, unsure how to voice the jumble of thoughts in my mind. An uncomfortable question sprung to mind. "Speaking of danger... Jake, what was Mr. Worthington really like? As your boss, I mean."

Jake's expression clouded, hesitating. "Mr. Worthington was a complicated man. Stern, demanding ... but also deeply passionate about the museum." His tone held a note of careful diplomacy. I tilted my head, sensing there was more left unsaid.

Jake sighed, running a hand through his hair. "Between us though ... the man could be a complete tyrant. Controlling, inflexible... He antagonized many people. I tried to stay out of his line of fire and just do my job." He shrugged. "Guess every workplace has its challenges. Why do you ask?"

I avoided eye contact, unsure how to voice my concern without revealing too much. "Just ... curious. Trying to get a better sense of how his employees felt towards him."

Jake's eyes clouded over for a moment before they quickly snapped back. "I'm more concerned with your feelings towards me."

Always the charmer.

I sighed, unsure how to voice the jumble of thoughts in my mind. "I won't deny this has been an unconventional start. My feelings are ... complicated." I tilted my head, regarding him thoughtfully.

My phone shattered the tender moment, ringing shrilly. I rummaged through my bag, checking the screen. It was Harry. My pulse quickened, wondering if he had somehow found out about our unauthorized visit to the museum this morning.

Jake tilted his head, reading my expression. "Looks like our secret is out." His tone held a note of worry. "Do you want me there when you speak to him?"

I sighed, wishing we had been more discreet. But lying to Harry now would only make things worse. I answered the call, bracing myself for the scolding I deserved.

"Harry, I was meaning to call you..."

His familiar voice was stern. "I just heard from the head of museum security about some 'enthusiastic patrons' triggering the alarms this morning. Do you know anything about that?"

My heart caught in my throat. "I can explain. We didn't mean any harm, we were just trying to find clues about..."

Harry cut me off with a weary sigh. "I don't want to hear it. Do you have any idea how much extra work you created for my team today?" His tone softened slightly. "Lola, I thought we agreed you would stop taking these unnecessary risks. I have enough real cases to handle without you creating new ones."

I ran a hand through my hair, feeling thoroughly chastened. "You're absolutely right, and I'm sorry. It won't happen again." An unpleasant thought struck me. "After the boardroom meeting ... no one else was hurt, were they?"

"Fortunately, no, thanks to the incompetence of the intruders, who I now know the identities of." Harry's tone was grim. "I don't want to have to start monitoring the museum security feeds for sightings of you as well as suspects, Lola. Promise me you'll stop this foolishness before I have to take official action."

My heart flopped like a fish out of water as his stern reprimand echoed in my ears. Guilt washed over me as I cast a sidelong glance at Jake, silently berating myself for ignoring his cautionary advice. Harry's professional tone on the call was a chilling reminder of the jovial back-and-forth we used to share. I mourned the lost warmth, the easy camaraderie, replaced by a rigid formality. When had our friendship turned so frosty?

Jake sidled up to me, his furrowed brows betraying his concern. "Sounded like a storm on the phone there. You okay?" he asked, his voice laced with empathetic worry.

I sighed, pushing a loose curl back from my face. "Just a stern wake-up call about my impulsiveness. And ... an unwelcome reminder of lost friendships." A wave of sentimentality swamped me, and I shook my head, trying to shake off the sudden sadness. "Jake, Harry was once my partner-in-crime. When did he transform into this stone-faced drill sergeant?"

Jake's expression melted into a sympathetic smile. "Change is life's only constant. But true friendships endure even when strained," he mused. "Maybe his sternness is just his clumsy way of showing concern for your well-being."

I laughed, though it lacked true mirth. "Sure, reprimands and veiled threats are definitely a peculiar way of expressing care. But I think you hit the nail on the head ... deep down, I believe he still has my back." I looked at Jake, my eyes shimmering with gratitude. "Besides, I've got new partners-in-crime who not only get my adventurous spirit but also join me in it."

Jake shot back a roguish grin. "Wouldn't miss our thrilling escapades for the world. But maybe we could hit the pause button on impromptu museum tours for now!"

"Perhaps," I said, a little nervously. Did that mean Jake didn't want a second date? The anticipation was killing me, but I didn't dare ask.

"So," Jake began, breaking the silence. "How about that second date? Maybe this time we can do something traditional ... like dinner. No museums involved."

I laughed, the tension easing. "As long as it's not in the museum cafeteria, I'm in."

He smiled, reaching over to gently squeeze my hand. "Deal. Now, let's finish this Turkish coffee before it gets cold."

Little did I know—our second date would never arrive.

Chapter 22

Heading into our local Italian haven, Giovanni's, I was all set to snatch up some comforting lasagna for dinner. As I swung the door open, the comforting, tomatoey warmth enveloped me. It was like being hugged by a giant, spicy meatball, a perfect antidote to the evening chill.

That comfort lasted precisely three seconds before I spotted Harry at the head of the queue. A jolt of surprise zipped through me. Seeing him out of his police-drama setup felt like spotting a teacher outside of school—an oddly disorienting experience.

Should I duck and make a run for it? But then again, that'd look guiltier than I actually was. Plus, I was way too hungry to abandon the lasagna mission. So, I braced myself and stepped up in line, praying for the conversational skills of a ninja.

"Lola," came the gruff voice I knew all too well. There went my cloak of invisibility.

"Harry," I countered, my voice aiming for casual. "What a coincidence! Or did you tap my phone for bistro surveillance, too?"

A moment of silence passed before Harry broke into a grin. "You're just lucky I'm off duty, otherwise I'd cite you for that sass."

I chuckled, relieved to see a flicker of the old Harry in his retort. "Guess we're even, then. You're getting ravioli, right?"

Harry looked surprised but nodded, his eyes thoughtful. "Excellent memory, Lola. Those late-night ravioli sessions after solving a tough case ... seems like another lifetime."

The wistful note in his voice caught me off guard. "Yes," I agreed softly, then tried to lighten the mood. "Here's hoping we don't have to revisit that with another museum fiasco, right?"

His stern façade was back as he picked up his order. "Exactly. Just remember our chat, alright?"

"Got it, Detective Sergeant Fun-killer," I saluted, feigning seriousness, and the corner of his mouth twitched upwards in an almost-smile.

"Watch it, Lola. Or I'll have to monitor your puns next," he quipped before exiting. As he turned to leave, he paused, then spun around, hesitation evident in his furrowed brow. "Lola, this Jake ... is he good to you?"

I was taken aback by his unexpected inquiry, but quickly recovered, grinning at him. "Why, Harry, are you jealous?"

He rolled his eyes at my teasing but didn't deny it. "Just don't want you getting hurt is all," he admitted, leaving me momentarily speechless.

As he exited Giovanni's, I couldn't help but smirk, the aftertaste of our banter mixing oddly with the tangy smell of the marinara sauce drifting in the air. Harry's uncharacteristic concern was as surprising as a well-done steak at a vegan gathering.

"But really, Harry, jealousy?" I mused aloud to the night air, picturing his classic 'I'd rather be doing paperwork' expression. He was always a wild card in the deck of my life, but this was a new suit altogether.

"Order for Lola!" The call snapped me from my thoughts. I was getting cold, and my stomach had started sending 'I'll-accept-pizza-as-a-substitute' signals. I dashed back to pick up my dinner, thanking the server and barely resisting the urge to tear into the lasagna right there. It smelled like what I imagined a hug from an Italian grandmother would feel like.

Outside, the evening was descending rapidly. Streetlights began to flicker on, casting long dancing shadows on the pavement. A brisk wind had picked up, sending a few dried leaves rustling down the street. It was the kind of night that begged for a warm blanket, a good book, and a lasagna rendezvous.

I started down the street, my pace brisk. As I passed Luigi's bakery, I caught sight of my reflection in the darkened window. There I was—Lola Hardgrave, still pretty new Gallery Café owner, full-time trouble magnet, carrying a lasagna like it was the crown jewels, and grinning like a Cheshire cat over a seemingly normal conversation with Detective Grumpy.

And what about Jake?

My mind raced. Jake or Harry? It was like deciding between chocolate and vanilla, each so different, yet enticing in their own ways.

Jake was the handsome security guard, with his constant, cheeky grin and quick wit. A charmer who could always make me laugh, even when I felt like tearing my hair out. But then, there was the matter of him potentially being a murder suspect. Talk about a wrinkle in the flirtation!

On the other hand, Harry was the detective, all brooding and business-like. He carried around a cloud of mystery like cologne, which added to his allure. Plus, he was grumpy in a way that was endearing.

We had a past, and it wasn't all sunshine and roses. But every time he frowned or looked at me with those piercing eyes, I felt a strange tingle.

I shook my head, trying to clear my thoughts. This was not a simple choice.

As my mind reeled, weighing the charm of Jake against the gruff reliability of Harry, I arrived at the outer door leading into the lobby of the apartments. I was just about to turn the key when I heard a rustling sound from behind. An involuntary shiver ran down my spine.

The glow from the nearby streetlight flickered, casting an eerie glow on my front door, but that wasn't what had me on edge. It was the distinct, unmistakable silhouette of a man standing there, hidden partially by the shadow of the large oak tree nearby.

I paused, my dinner now forgotten. The man's features were indistinguishable, but the stance ... it was familiar. Suddenly, my cozy evening seemed light-years away.

As I took a tentative step closer, the figure stepped into the light, and my heart nearly stopped.

Standing at my door was neither Harry nor Jake, but the last person I expected to see...

Chapter 23

Victor.

In place of his usual commanding presence, sharply tailored suit, and booming voice was a man in faded jeans and a nondescript jacket, his features shadowed with worry.

"Victor?" I stuttered, my voice teetering on the edge of surprise. The sight of him on my doorstep was as unexpected as finding a cat at a dog show. "What brings you here?"

His stare, usually so formidable, held a flicker of uncertainty. "We need to have a bit of a chat, Lola," he murmured, his voice edged with urgency.

I hesitated, startled by his sudden appearance and the drastic change in his demeanor. But his serious expression was persuasive. "Alright, come in," I conceded, unlocking the door with a sigh.

We made our way up to the apartment in silence. The moment Victor crossed the threshold of my usually cheery living space, the air seemed to change, replaced by a tension that you could almost slice with a butter knife. He swept his eyes over my apartment, finally landing on me with a serious look that was a far cry from his regular cocky grin.

"Are you alone?" he questioned. His words sent my pulse into overdrive.

"Why are you here, Victor?" My voice had a tremble, a testament to my unease. This was not the domineering museum curator who would order others around like a general on the battlefield. This man was a stranger.

He met my gaze, pausing briefly as if choosing his words carefully. "There's more to all this than meets the eye, Lola," he confessed, his words hanging in the air laced with suspense.

"What do you mean?" My voice wobbled as I asked, trying to maintain my composure.

"Before the two murders, strange things had been happening at the museum recently. Records have been deleted from the archives in the inventory software." His eyes held a mix of emotions I couldn't quite pinpoint. "At first, I thought it was just carelessness or technical glitches. But it's too frequent and too specific to be random."

He leaned in slightly, his voice dropping to a conspiratorial whisper. "The Johnston artifacts, the ones connected to Worthington's family history—someone's taken an unusual interest in those pieces lately. I reviewed the access logs, Lola. The same unauthorized access code was used each time. I have no way of knowing who used that code. And the altered records..." He swallowed hard; his expression was severe. "They were all related to the same era that Worthington's ancestors were active in."

Victor stared at me, his warning clear. "Someone knows about your personal connection. They're toying with us, trying to throw us off the scent. I don't know who yet or why, but this is far from an ordinary case of museum vandalism." His voice took on a note of grim urgency.

"Watch your step, Lola. They've already invaded our digital archives. Your home may be next."

"Victor—what?"

He swallowed hard, his expression severe, anxious. "Just be careful, Lola," he insisted, his usually commanding voice now laced with genuine concern. "Be very, very careful." And with no further explanation and not giving me a chance to ask questions or say anything else, Victor got up and fled the apartment.

The initial thrill of Victor's sudden visit dissolved, replaced by a creeping unease that turned my stomach. My living room became a pacing ground as I replayed our past conversations. The pieces of this mystery were growing in number but not assembling easily. The current obscure picture was no calming Monet. Deciding it was time to loop Jake into this development, I dialed his number, my fingers trembling slightly. We needed to review everything we thought we knew about this investigation, considering Victor's unsettling disclosure.

Jake picked up on the second ring. "Lola? Everything alright?"

"Jake," I managed to say, my voice revealing my unease, "Victor popped by for a surprise visit."

A pause. "What?" Jake blurted, surprise and concern threading through his tone. "What on earth did he say?"

I recounted the strange encounter with Victor, right down to his cryptic warning. The silence from Jake was deafening, lasting a few heartbeats before he finally found his voice.

"We need to meet. ASAP."

I nodded to myself, "We should bring Polly in as well," I added, "She should be in the loop about this."

An hour later, we convened at the Gallery Café, our usual sanctuary now shrouded in the gravity of our midnight rendezvous. Even Jake's usually irrepressible humor seemed muted that night. We gathered around the sturdy oak table that I'd spent countless childhood summers polishing with my uncle. Our hands sought comfort around warm coffee mugs, each holding the special blend that was a proud signature of the Gallery Café. I wished, not for the first time, that the brew could also dissolve the knot of apprehension growing in my chest. Jake kicked off the conversation. "Let's put everything on the table. Victor's warning, the targeted artifacts... It all ties back to his peculiar behavior at the museum."

Polly's brows scrunched together in deep thought, mirroring the look she usually had while lost in her art, her fingers itching to draw out the problem instead of just talking about it. "But why drop this bomb on Lola? What's his game?"

"Could he be trying to send us on a wild goose chase?" I suggested. "A diversion tactic, maybe?"

Jake scratched his stubbled chin thoughtfully. "Might be, but wouldn't that just put him in the spotlight? He's savvy enough to see that."

We tossed around theories, our conversation resembling one of Polly's abstract paintings—full of twists, turns, and vibrant ideas, but somehow lacking that last stroke to bring it all together. Suddenly, Jake's eyes widened with realization. "Hang on. Wasn't Marcella the one with access to Victor's office?"

Jake's words fell like the drop of paint that suddenly makes a picture clear. Polly's eyes met mine, and I could see the dawning understanding there, the same look she had when an art piece finally came together in her mind.

"The idea of Marcella manipulating Victor isn't far-fetched," Polly voiced out, her expression reflecting the gravity of this potential breakthrough. "He could be a pawn in her scheme."

"Hold your horses," Jake cut in, eyes dancing with mischief. "Marcella? Too easy. She might as well have a blinking neon sign saying 'I'm the bad guy'."

Polly and I both blinked at him. "What do you mean, Jake?" Polly asked, her eyebrows knitting together in confusion.

"Think about it," Jake said, tapping his coffee mug thoughtfully. "If Victor's being played, wouldn't he likely realize if Marcella, his close colleague and cousin, was the one pulling the strings?"

There was something in his tone that caught my attention. It was too measured, too calculated. I eyed him, my thoughts whirling.

"Jake," I started, my voice barely a whisper, "You work at the museum too. Are you suggesting one of your own colleagues and not a family member ... could be a suspect?"

His eyes met mine, a flicker of something undefinable crossing his face. "It's a possibility. Marcella could be a red herring, a distraction from the real puppeteer."

The room fell silent as the implications of his words seeped in. If Jake was right, we were indeed back at square one, with a faceless enemy skulking in the shadows.

Jake's expression darkened. "I don't want to believe it," he said quietly. "But we can't rule anything out." He sighed, rubbing the back of his neck. "Yes, Polly. As much as I hate to say it... including me."

Jake held her gaze, and in that moment, I saw a flicker of fear behind his eyes. The thought of himself as a suspect clearly disturbed him.

Uncertainty curled around us, getting cozier with the smell of freshly roasted coffee.

"But with a difference," I pointed out, my mind working overtime. "We now know someone at the museum is involved. Does that make finding the murderer easier or harder?"

"Good question," Jake agreed, his face a hard mask of determination. "Tomorrow, we pay closer attention to everyone at the museum. No exceptions."

I cast a furtive glance at Jake. His relaxed posture belied the gravity of his words.

"Don't worry, I've been practicing my innocent face in the mirror." I smiled, but on the inside my heart sank as I considered the facts. Jake's position at the museum gave him access and means. I didn't want to believe it, but...

Jake cleared his throat, rising abruptly from the table. "I should get going," he said, his usual casual demeanor noticeably absent. "Early day tomorrow at the museum. Lots of... observing to do."

He didn't meet my eyes as he shrugged on his coat and stalked out of the café. Polly watched him go with a frown, before turning to me.

"What aren't you telling me, Lola?" she asked, her voice gentle but firm. "You have your 'we need cocoa and contemplation' face on. Spill the beans! There's more to this than Jake just being a suspect in theory, isn't there?"

I stared down into the dregs of my coffee, my throat tight. With Jake gone, there was no reason to hide the truth from my closest friend. "Polly, I-I'm afraid Jake may actually be involved," I confessed, the words tumbling out in a rush. "He has means, motive, and the way he was acting..."

Polly's sharp intake of breath showed she grasped the implications immediately. But when I finally met her eyes, they were full of sympathy and concern rather than shock or judgment.

"I know how close you two are," she said, reaching over to squeeze my hand. "I know romantic entanglements with suspects are frowned upon in the detective handbook, but the heart wants what it wants!" Her expression softened. "But this is serious, Lola. We have to consider every possibility, as ugly as they might be." She paused, her face etched in thought. "Jake's position at the museum is troubling, I'll admit. But do we have any hard evidence yet that points directly at him?"

I shook my head, feeling a wave of frustration and despair. "No, just speculation, but"—

"Then we keep an open mind," Polly interjected firmly. "Make note of anything unusual involving Jake, but don't confront him until we have proof. We owe him that much." Her expression softened. "And we owe it to you too, to be absolutely certain before making an accusation that could ruin a friendship—or a budding romance."

We left the café in a fog of exhaustion and uncertainty. But as Polly approached our door, she turned to me with an expression caught between hesitation and hope.

"Lola, before we call it a night... I have one more idea."

I paused with my key in the lock, pulse quickening. "What is it, Polly?"

She took a deep breath. "The puppeteer has been toying with us because they feel in control. What if we could turn the tables?"

My eyes widened as I caught her meaning. "You mean ... set a trap?"

Polly nodded, eyes glinting with determination. "We've been reacting this whole time. It's time we forced their hand. If we dangle the right bait, the puppeteer won't be able to resist coming out from behind the curtain."

I felt a spark of adrenaline at the thought of finally taking action rather than scrambling to keep up. But with it came fear of the unknown. "It's risky, Polly. Once we draw them out ... there's no going back."

Chapter 24

"Setting a trap? This is crazy." My words echoed louder than I would have liked off the marble walls of the Fawnwood Museum, painting an eerily surreal picture against the solemn stillness, as we were the only ones in this room. I had slept on this trap idea and now wasn't so sure. "Polly, we're about as qualified to be secret agents as your Aunt Edna's poodle."

Polly gave me a stern look. The glow from the display lights reflected in her determined eyes. "Lola, we're the only ones standing between our town's history and a manipulative, invisible puppeteer. We need to step up."

Her confidence was infectious, although the knot of anxiety in my stomach tightened.

The marble statues seemed to listen in, their stone eyes appearing just as skeptical as I felt. But seeing Polly's iron resolve made me catch a glimmer of her infectious confidence. Despite the knot of anxiety in my belly, I exhaled, my eyes drifting over the rows of artifacts that bore silent witness to our town's vibrant history. "Alright," I conceded, shoulders squaring. "So, what's our grand scheme, 'Agent Polly'?"

A triumphant smile warmed her face, sparking a new courage within me. She pulled a small, dog-eared notebook from her bag and flipped through pages of jumbled notes and sketches. "Every brilliant plan needs irresistible bait."

Our plan unfolded on the wooden bench beside the Native American exhibit, a reminder of the vibrant history we were striving to protect. We dug into our notes, scrutinizing each detail of our investigation to find the perfect lure.

"The Johnston artifacts," I murmured, remembering Victor's suspicions about their importance to our hidden enemy.

Polly's pencil stopped mid-sketch. "We could stage a special exhibit, unveil a 'newly discovered' Johnston artifact. The prospect of a fresh treasure might be irresistible."

A chill swept over me, goosebumps prickling on my skin. We were walking a tightrope, one misstep away from alerting the puppeteer to our plan, yet I felt invigorated. We were moving forward, taking the fight to them.

"After Victor's mysterious visit the other night I really don't think he is responsible for the death of Worthington or Brittany. I think Victor needs to be in on this if we have any hope of pulling it off," I pointed out, remembering his crucial role as the museum curator. "He can help us make the exhibit believable."

Polly glanced at me, a question in her eyes. "And Jake?"

My heart pounded at his name. Jake, who was still a puzzle we hadn't solved. "Yes, Jake too," I agreed. "We have to keep an eye on everyone."

Our hushed voices, along with the scratch of Polly's pencil against her notebook, echoed through the museum's hallowed halls. By the time we had plotted our course, a sense of determination filled me, transforming our anxiety into steely resolve.

"Are you ready, Polly?" I asked, a hint of apprehension slipping through.

Polly shot me a resolute nod following her words. "Let's end this, Lola. Let's unmask this puppeteer."

I managed a small, reassured smile.

Our plan was audacious, daring, and honestly, a little reckless. But it was all we had. Victor, the seasoned museum curator, was our first hurdle. If he didn't buy into our idea, it would be impossible to proceed. So, we scheduled a meeting with him, under the guise of discussing new community engagement initiatives.

The next day, we found ourselves in Victor's office, a room filled with artifacts and the faint smell of old books. Victor sat behind his desk, his sharp eyes studying us over the rim of his glasses but not revealing anything about the conversation he and I had just a couple of nights ago.

"We have a proposition," I began, my voice steady despite the fluttering in my stomach. "We want to set a trap for the puppeteer."

Victor's eyebrows shot up, but he didn't interrupt. I took a deep breath and continued, "We want to stage a special exhibit, unveil a 'newly discovered' Johnston artifact. We believe the prospect of a fresh treasure might be irresistible to your puppeteer."

Victor leaned back in his chair, his expression thoughtful. "That's a bold move," he said after a moment. "And risky. Lola, I warned you to be careful... This is not being careful."

"We know," Polly chimed in, her voice firm. "But we're not getting anywhere playing defense. We need to take control of the game."

Victor studied us for a long moment, his gaze flicking between our determined faces. Finally, he sighed and reached into a drawer, pulling out a key. "In the basement, there's a replica of a Johnston artifact. I've kept it stored away for years. You can use it for your ... exhibit."

Relief washed over me, and I exchanged a triumphant look with Polly.

Victor's support was crucial, and we had it. Now it was time to set our plan in motion. But there was another piece to this puzzle that we couldn't ignore.

"I guess we need to find Jake?" I asked, my voice barely above a whisper and no longer confident we should tell him our plan. The question hung in the air, heavy with unspoken implications.

Polly looked at me, her eyes softening. "We monitor him, Lola. But maybe we don't let him in on our plan just yet, or at least not the entire purpose behind the plan."

A pang of guilt twisted in my stomach. Jake, with his serene smile and warm eyes, was again a potential suspect. The thought of him being involved in this mess was like a punch to the gut. But I couldn't let my personal feelings cloud my judgment. We were in this to protect our town's history, and if Jake was involved, we needed to find out.

I nodded, swallowing the lump in my throat. "Alright," I agreed, my voice steady. "We monitor Jake, but we don't let him in on our plot."

We knew we needed more hands on deck to set up the exhibit. So, we turned to a few trusted friends and volunteers, spinning them a tale of a surprise, historical exhibit meant to boost town spirit. Their enthusiasm was infectious, and with their help, we could get the permissions and materials for our 'special exhibit.'

We decided that the Gallery Café would cater another evening, opening the exhibit, making a big deal out of the new discovery and even using the guise of honoring the memory of Joseph Worthington.

With Victor's keys to the museum, we had unrestricted access to the sprawling structure, even during the odd hours when the museum was usually deserted. It felt strange, manipulating our close-knit community this way. But, we assured each other, it was all for a noble cause. We were, after all, fighting for our town's history.

It took some time and planning, but the opening of the exhibit was coming together. With everything falling into place, we found ourselves one afternoon heaving a large crate onto the stage next to a pedestal in the center of the museum's most regal gallery. Our plan was in motion.

"Good grief, this crate weighs more than an elephant," grumbled Polly, her face flushed with effort as she helped me heave the container housing the supposed 'Johnston artifact' into place. The cavernous space of the Fawnwood Museum echoed with our grunts and the scraping of wood against stone.

"Makes you wonder how Victor managed all this by himself all these years," I huffed in agreement. "To bad Jake had the day off. He could have done all this grunt work for us." We straightened, dusting our hands on our pants and surveying our work with satisfaction. "Of course, he didn't have to do this lifting himself." I added. The heavy crate, encased in swathes of protective padding, looked every bit the part of a mysterious, newly discovered artifact.

A sudden clatter had us both spinning around, eyes wide. My heart pounded as I saw a broom fall over, handle bouncing against the floor. We exchanged a glance, our smiles fading into nervous tension.

"Calm down, Lola. It's just a broom," Polly chided, though her voice quivered slightly. It seemed the museum's shadowy corners held more than just historic relics tonight.

We returned to our work, unpacking a beautiful statue of a man and a woman holding hands, looking off in the distance as if looking at a beautiful sunset or possibly a full moon. Once the statue was perfectly placed, we went about laying out the velvet ropes to mark a path around the artifact's display. The museum, usually a place of quiet reflection and learning, now felt more like a stage set for a spy thriller. I could almost imagine a secret agent descending from the ceiling, just like in the movies.

But this was no Hollywood production, and we weren't professional detectives. Each time the old building creaked or a distant car alarm sounded, I jumped. Every footfall seemed amplified, a potential threat. The paranoia was as thick as the dust in the temporally closed gallery we were setting up. I half expected to find a mummy lurking in a corner.

"Should we... I don't know ... set up some sort of surveillance?" I proposed, my eyes darting around the lofty space.

Polly scratched her chin thoughtfully. "Might be a good idea. We can't be here 24/7, and during the opening party we can't see every-where ourselves." We agreed to set up a few hidden cameras, aiming them at the statue, the entrance, and possible hiding spots. It was a rudimentary system, but it would have to do.

Suddenly, a harsh siren-like sound blared from Polly's purse. We both let out yelps of surprise, clutching our chests. Fishing her phone out, Polly looked at the screen and groaned, "False alarm. Just a security system ad. Turned up my volume by accident."

Exhaling, I laughed a bit too forcefully. "Well, at least we know our hearts are in good shape."

Our laughter filled the museum room, bouncing off the high ceilings and marble walls.

The stage was set. The trap was in place. And we were ready.

Chapter 25

The museum hummed with visitors of all types. Unlike the masquerade ball, this event was open to one and all. We had prepared a simple spread across several tables of finger sandwiches, mints, fruit trays and vegetable trays and, of course, coffee and tea. We tried to keep it simple while also making it at least somewhat elegant.

There was too much planning and activity not to tell Jake something, but we stuck by the story we told everyone else. Trying to honor the memory of Mr. Worthington with a little event to put this newly discovered Johnston artifact on display. Shortly after the event was opened to the public, Jake walked in. He was in his uniform, so he was on duty, but he stopped and chatted with us briefly. I was cheery and gave him a sweet smile as I handed a cup of tea to a visitor. Jake soon headed out again, saying he had to make his rounds.

The next few hours were uneventful. Many people filed through the now reopened room of the museum enjoying the new display and the food provided. We saw many of our friends, people who had been to the Café, and several owners of other shops around town. We saw many people we didn't know, but no one looked out of place or suspicious in any way. It also didn't seem like anyone realized this was not a genuine Johnston artifact, but then, it would take a very keen eye to see that.

As we packed up the leftovers, what few there were, and cleaned up, I asked Polly, "Do you think this was all a waste of time?"

"I think it is too soon to tell. Maybe, but whoever has such a keen interest in the Johnston collection may not have wanted to be exposed to so many people. I have a feeling that it sparked interest, and, if nothing else, I think we gave the museum and the town a little boost."

"You're probably right. I guess for now, we leave the cameras in place and monitor for the next few days." I lamented.

The museum seemed to hold its breath as we watched the monitors, waiting for anyone who might fall into this trap we carefully laid out. The vast, brightly lit gallery we were monitoring now felt cramped and claustrophobic as we sat hidden away in Brittany's unused office, eyes glued to the various camera feeds we had set up. Although the museum had its own cameras, we had been careful to keep these cameras and their locations a secret, even from Victor and Jake. If anyone showed up, they wouldn't know they were being watched.

Polly kept nervously fiddling with the zoom function, causing the image on the screen to distort and blur. I shot her an irritable glance. "Will you stop that? You're making me dizzy."

She grimaced apologetically. "Sorry, I'm just restless. How long have we been stuck in this art-filled sardine can?"

I checked my watch. "Over two hours. Whoever we're waiting for sure is taking their sweet time."

Polly sighed, running a hand through her short blonde pixie cut. "Maybe no one is coming. What if this was all for naught?"

The thought wiped the smile from my face. What if we had been wrong? What if we had miscalculated somehow? But then I remembered the careful steps we had taken to ensure the secrecy of our plan. "We've been careful, Polly," I reassured her, "We installed the cameras ourselves, remember? We didn't even tell Victor or Jake where they were."

As doubt crept in, a flicker of movement caught my eye on the monitor. I squinted at the screen, blood turning to ice. A figure had appeared, striding purposefully towards the Johnston artifact exhibit.

Polly gasped. "Someone's here!"

We peered closer, holding our breaths. The figure's features were obscured, their face hidden in the shadows. They approached the crate, glancing around furtively before finally dipping into the soft light.

I let out an involuntary cry.

"Jake?!"

He stood in front of the artifact, an unreadable expression on his face as he reached out to touch the statue.

Polly shot me a bewildered glance. "Jake? But why would he..." Her voice trailed off into uncertain silence.

I was speechless, anger and betrayal rising like bile within me.Jake... Jake, who I had trusted against my better judgment. Jake, with his roguish grin and careless charm. How could I have been so foolish?

Polly touched my arm gently. "Lola... there has to be an explanation. He is on duty. Maybe he is doing his normal rounds." Though her voice wavered with doubt.

And then Jake scanned the room before pulling something out of his pocket - a small electronic device. He attached it close to one of the hidden cameras, causing the feed to go briefly fuzzy before reconnecting.

I gasped. "A signal jammer!"

The new suspicion was mounting faster than I could process, yet a small part of me still clung to hope. Jake must have a reason for placing that device that made sense. He had to. Maybe it is part of their security procedure?

Jake exited the gallery, striding purposefully out of the door. He disappeared from view, leaving us in stunned silence. I couldn't shake off the feeling that Jake was acting under duress. His usual easygoing demeanor was replaced with a tense, almost a desperate air.

Finally, Polly spoke. "Should we confront him?"

A thousand emotions warred within me—anger, confusion, hurt. In the end, it was a determination that rose above the rest.

"No," I said firmly. "Not yet. We need answers, and we won't get them from a surprised Jake." I took a deep, steadying breath. "We follow him. Quietly. And we see what he is up to."

Polly nodded, fire in her green eyes. "For answers. And for justice."

We slipped out of Brittany's abandoned office, retracing Jake's path through the museum halls. Each step dredged up memories - our first meeting, late night texts, his carefree laugh. I clung to those moments, hoping against hope they were not built on lies.

Rounding the corner, we spotted Jake exiting through a side door out into the gardens. We quietly made our way outside, the cool night air caressing our cheeks. The moonlit hedges cast twisted shadows across our path as we crept behind a stately elm, watching Jake pace back and forth.

"What's he waiting for?" Polly whispered.

A figure appeared from the darkness, striding purposefully towards Jake. My heart leaped into my throat—the clipboard, the thin mustache ... it was Victor.

They stood together in hushed conversation for a few tense moments before Jake handed over an envelope. Victor pocketed it hastily, casting furtive glances around him before retreating into the museum.

Jake lit a cigarette, features grim and tight. He took a long drag before letting out a heavy sigh, muttering aloud to himself. "This had better be worth it..."

Beside me, Polly gasped. A twig snapped beneath her foot, punctuating the silence.

Jake whirled around, eyes wide. Our eyes locked for a split second before he bolted, slipping into the night.

I pulled out my phone with shaking hands, dialing the one person I knew we could trust.

"Harry, it's me. We need your help."

Chapter 26

"Isn't it a lovely evening for a stroll?" Harry remarked, his tone dry as we crunched along the pebbled path of the museum gardens. His comment was so out of character that I let out a short laugh.

"Harry," I retorted, rolling my eyes at his attempt at levity. "We have a mystery to solve, remember?"

Harry glanced at me from under raised eyebrows. "And pacing like caged beasts will accomplish that, how?" His voice was gruff, but there was a twinkle in his eye that softened his words. "Humor me, Lola. We've got all night. And besides, it's been a while since I've seen you like this. "

His comment made me pause. Was he referring to the tension that had always simmered between us? The unspoken 'what ifs' that had lingered in the air whenever we were together? I sighed, deciding to play along with his unusual mood. After all, this was the closest we'd ever come to a date. The garden really was beautiful, lanterns casting a soft glow over the winding paths, the murmur and chirp of nocturnal creatures lending the space a symphonic quality. An owl hooted, startling a nearby nightingale into song.

Despite the picturesque surroundings, my thoughts refused to stray from what we had witnessed. Jake's furtive behavior. The envelope handed to Victor. What role did they play in our puppeteer's scheme?

Polly walked alongside us, her silence a testament to how troubled she was. Her usual cheerful, upbeat nature had been dampened—a stark reminder of our precarious situation.

At last, Harry spoke. "So, run me through everything again. Slowly this time."

I sighed, recounting the details of our discovery, our trap with Victor's help, and then Jake's involvement with Victor. Polly added her observations, her voice tinged with both confusion and concern. This new wrinkle in the mystery only complicated the web of deceit we found ourselves ensnared in.

Harry's thoughtful silence when we finished speaking spoke volumes. There were pieces to this puzzle that even he had not expected. For all his gruffness, Harry possessed a keen mind and uncommon intuition - qualities that had served him well during his years as a detective. Perhaps now they could help us unravel this murky mystery.

"I'll admit, this new development with Jake is troubling," Harry said at last. "Although we must be careful not to rush to judgment. Motive and opportunity do not necessarily equate to guilt."

His words, though reasonable, grated against my growing distrust of Jake. At my sullen silence, Harry continued.

"For now, we observe quietly and gather as much information as possible. The truth, when it arises, will catch us unawares, as truths often do." His steady eyes met mine. "Can you wait patiently for it, Lola?"

His wise words settled something within me, lighting a small candle of hope amidst the darkness of doubt and suspicion. I managed a small smile. "When did you become the voice of reason, Harry?"

He smirked. "It must be old age finally settling in."

Polly piped up then, wincing apologetically. "Not to interrupt this heartwarming 'moment', but what's our next move? We've still got a puppeteer to catch."

"Right you are," Harry said, sobering. "And I have an idea."

We gathered around as he shared his plan in hushed tones beneath the great elm, our faces catching the flickering lantern light. Though the approaching dawn had yet to break, I felt a stirring of hope within - faint, but determined. Mysteries blurred the truth, but patience and wisdom could guide us through the lingering fog. And, I thought wryly, a dash of good, old-fashioned sleuthing wouldn't hurt either.

With a purposeful stride, the three of us made our way back into the museum, our goal now clear—discover the puppeteer's identity and end their game, once and for all. Harry led the way, while Polly and I fell into step behind him, a growing sense of determination swelling within our chests.

As we canvassed the library and galleries for clues, I allowed myself to wonder absently who this mysterious manipulator truly was. Had we overlooked something vital? What remained obscured?

Our search yielded no new information, serving only to increase our determination. At last, we stood regrouping in the atrium, frustration simmering just below the surface.

Harry frowned. "It seems our opponent remains a step ahead."

I was ready to give up when Polly spoke up, a clenched fist raised in determination. "We will find them, Lola. The truth is out there, we just have to keep looking!"

"Agreed," Harry said, a new spark in his eye. "Our puppeteer won't stay hidden forever. They're smart, but we're smarter. We have a knack for uncovering the truth, and we won't stop until we do. For now, however, the museum will open soon, and I am exhausted. I know you two have to be as well. Let's go get some rest and clear our heads. Let's meet back here at eight this evening when the museum closes and resume our mission."

Encouraged, I nodded. "Alright. I think you are right. I can hardly think any longer." We will see you here at eight o'clock."

The security guard on duty let us in before locking the doors behind us. Harry had explained to him what we needed to do. Rested and ready to go, I said. "Let's get back to it. We can't give up now. Not when we're so close."

We dispersed once again, turning the museum upside down in our search for clues. Hours passed as we scanned old newspaper clippings, reread emails, and studied security footage. We ran into dead ends, false leads, and more questions than answers, but our resolve never faltered.

As we moved through the rooms, my mind spun back through my memories of Jake. Every smile, every kind gesture, now seemed suspect. Every conversation felt tainted with his potential betrayal. The questions whirled in my mind: Why would Jake be involved in this? What did Victor have to do with it if he helped us set the trap?

Shaking off my doubts, I refocused my efforts on uncovering the truth. This was bigger than my feelings for Jake. If he was involved, we had to find out. If not for us, then for the town and for the history that was at risk.

As the night wore on, the museum took on an eerie quiet. The only sounds were the shuffling of our feet and the occasional creaking of the old building settling. Our search grew more desperate as the hours ticked by with no new leads.

Just as we were about to call it a night, Polly let out a triumphant shout from the other end of the museum. Harry and I shot each other a look before rushing towards her.

Polly stood in front of a painting of the town's founder, her finger pointing at the corner of the frame. "Look!" she said, excitement evident in her voice. "A hidden compartment!"

Harry examined it closely. "Well, I'll be..." he said, a smirk playing on his lips. "It seems we've got our next clue."

As we opened the hidden compartment, we found a note, the handwriting painfully familiar. It was Jake's. The note was short and cryptic, hinting at a meeting spot. The words were vague, but the implication was clear: Jake was involved in something he didn't want us to know about.

Polly and I exchanged a look. Our discovery was both thrilling and alarming. It brought us one step closer to uncovering the puppeteer, but it also confirmed our worst fears about Jake.

Harry pocketed the note, determination hardening his features. "I'll take this to the station and run it through some tests. We can't be sure it's Jake's handwriting until we get it analyzed."

As the morning sun crept over the horizon, we decided we had had enough. As I trudged home, a mixture of dread and anticipation gnawed at me. We were closer than ever to catching the puppeteer, but the cost seemed too high. Could I really bear to see Jake behind bars?

My sleep was troubled, my dreams filled with images of Jake and Victor, conspiring against us. I woke after only a few hours sleep, the day ahead filled with both hope and trepidation. Would we finally catch the puppeteer today? Would we be able to prove Jake's innocence or guilt?

With these thoughts in mind, I made my way back to the museum. Today was the day. Today, we would finally unmask the puppeteer.

Once again, the 3 of us met at the museum. It felt different in the light of day—the secrets of the night had faded into the fluorescent glow. Our footsteps echoed in the spacious atrium as we made our way to Victor's office, discussing last night's discoveries in hushed tones.

Harry led the way, an air of quiet confidence about him. "The handwriting expert should be able to verify if the note belongs to Jake," he said. "That, along with the security footage, will finally give us concrete proof."

I wanted so badly for the note not to be Jake's, hoping against hope he had an innocent explanation. But evidence pointed otherwise, no matter how much it stung.

Polly rested a comforting hand on my shoulder. "We have to be prepared for any outcome, for the truth to surprise us." Her words held a wisdom beyond her years, forged in the furnace of her creative spirit.

Approaching Victor's office, we found the door hanging ajar. My pulse quickened. Before we could react, a figure emerged carrying a stack of files.

Victor froze upon seeing us. "What are you doing here?" he demanded, face flushed.

Harry ignored his tone. "We need to speak with you. In private." Victor hesitated, then gestured for us to follow. We entered his office, Harry locking the door behind us. "We know about the note Jake gave you," Harry said, his tone hard. "The envelope, with a payment of some sort, I am guessing. What were you two scheming?"

Victor's eyes narrowed. "Are you spying on me? Spying and breaking and entering are serious offenses, you know."

"Answer the question," Harry pressed.

Victor blew out a sigh. "I caught Jake copying some records. Threatened to expose him unless he paid me to keep quiet." He shrugged. "Nothing sinister, just a bit of extortion between coworkers and relatives."

I absorbed Victor's words, a glimmer of hope sparking in my chest. If the note was simply a blackmail payment, perhaps Jake was innocent after all.

Harry was the first to break the silence, his voice steady and authoritative. "Victor, we need to understand what's going on. You need to tell us everything."

Victor shifted uncomfortably in his chair, his eyes darting between us. "I've told you everything I know," he insisted, his voice strained.

Harry leaned forward, his trained eyes never leaving Victor. "And the note Jake gave you? The payment?"

Victor's eyes flickered with something I couldn't quite place. Fear? Guilt? "I told you, it was just a … misunderstanding. Nothing more."

Harry wasn't convinced. He pressed further, his questions sharp and probing. But Victor remained evasive, his answers vague and unsatisfactory. His body language was defensive, his arms crossed tightly over his chest, his eyes avoiding ours.

After what felt like hours, Harry finally leaned back in his chair, a deep sigh escaping his lips. His face was hard, his jaw set in a grim line. "Alright, Victor. We're done here. For now."

We left Victor's office, the door closing with a soft click behind us. The silence in the hallway was deafening, the tension palpable. We had questioned Victor, pushed him for answers, but had come away with nothing. No evidence, no leads, just more questions.

As I lay in bed that night, Victor's words echoed in my mind. He claimed Jake had only paid him off, yet something about his story didn't add up.

A supposed "blackmail payment" did not fit with Jake's behavior at the museum. There had to be more to his involvement. I decided to pay Jake a visit in the morning, to see if I could catch him in a lie and get to the truth.

"Jake, we need to talk." I got straight to the point, watching carefully for his reaction.

He sighed. "Lola, I know this all looks bad. But I promise there's an explanation."

Listening to his story, certain details didn't match up. He claimed not to know anything about copying records at the museum, yet had paid Victor off? I caught him in a lie, finally confronting him with the truth.

Jake's façade cracked, admitting to his role but insisting he wasn't working alone. "Victor's involved too," he revealed. "We share something in common—a secret that threatens to destroy us both."

Chapter 27

Jake shifted uncomfortably in his seat, his hands fidgeting with the edge of the table. His eyes, usually so full of charm and warmth, were clouded with a seriousness I had rarely seen. He gave me a look suggesting he was about to spill secrets he'd been holding onto for a long time.

"It started years ago," he began, his words measured, "when my grandfather, Elias, was running the museum. He and Victor were thicker than thieves. After the fire, Worthington forced my grandfather out and took control. But that wasn't enough for him. He began embezzling funds, pinching artifacts to sell in secret, threatening to sell off my family's land to line his own pockets."

I felt a realization dawning. "So, that's why you wanted to help us—you wanted justice for your grandfather and the wrongs Worthington committed."

Jake nodded reluctantly. "We had to protect our mission. Not just for my grandfather, but for Victor. Worthington made his life miserable, too. We've been gathering evidence for years to expose him."

I knitted my brows. "But why pin the murders on Marcella instead of just coming clean?"

Jake exhaled, dragging a hand through his hair in exasperation. "There was too much at stake. If we came forward outright, Worthington would bury us. Framing Marcella seemed the only way to stop him without jeopardizing everything."

There was still one part of the puzzle that didn't fit. "Why drag me into all this, Jake? You could have been honest from the start."

"I needed an ally. Someone clever enough to help us navigate this maze. But you're right, Lola, I should never have deceived you. I thought I was protecting you, protecting our cause. I was wrong." His voice was soft, filled with remorse.

Suddenly, everything clicked into place... "That's why you guided me to Marcella that night at the museum," I realized. "You wanted me to catch her snooping."

Jake nodded, looking like he'd swallowed a bug. "I had noticed Marcella creeping around the museum, looking like she was up to no good. When she pointed a finger at Brittany for the murder post-haste, I was sure she was trying to deflect suspicion."

"And the barn?" I prodded.

Jake paused, took a deep breath, then admitted, "Planned by Victor. We wanted to steer the investigation."

"What about the threats? The SUV chase? I mean, it really was Marcella in that car." I asked, my voice hitting an octave higher in disbelief.

Jake looked at me apologetically. "I didn't know he would go to that extent, Lola. I truly didn't. Victor told Marcella that you and Polly were going to try to stop the demolition of that barn. She wanted it down because she thought it was an eyesore on her land and she had plans for world class stables. So, she didn't want anything to stop the barn coming down."

I swallowed, taking it all in. "We have to go to Harry with the truth, Jake. No more games."

For the first time since we began the conversation, Jake seemed relieved. "You're right, Lola. Let's do this. For my grandfather, and for us."

Chapter 28

Fawnwood, a quirky little town right out of a jigsaw puzzle, huddled amid rolling green hills and babbling brooks—the kind of place where city folks fled to 'get away from it all'. It was the dictionary definition of quaint, with an added bonus of the Whispering Willows Spa, the town's major selling point. As the spa's oaken door swung closed behind us, I felt the outside world being sucked away, like a bad mood in a chick flick. It was a sanctuary where manicures met tranquility.

Bathed in hues of serenity, with calming background tunes playing hide-and-seek among the lavender-scented air, the spa could very well double as the secret headquarters of Zen. Polly, ever the pampering evangelist, had railroaded us into this. "Lola," she'd stated in that bossy older sister tone, "you've been looking like a zombie this past week, you need some relaxation."

Nestled in overly plush recliners, our feet swishing in soapy Jacuzzi waters, I felt the knots in my shoulders uncoil. Across from me, Polly was busy chatting up a storm with the manicurist, her laughter effervescing like the champagne in our glasses. The gal never let a mystery get in the way of a good spa day.

Eventually, the dreaded Jake topic bobbed to the surface. Polly, looking like a beauty-masked superhero, caught my eyes, her voice dropping a notch. "Spill the beans on your Jake encounter," she prompted, "and don't you dare skim."

Exhaling, I paused for a theatrical sip of the champagne, buying time. "Where to even start?" I mumbled and launched into the tale of the early morning Jakey confession. Polly was a champ, offering no interruptions as I shared Jake's convoluted involvement and Victor's double-crossing ways. Her eyebrows made a few surprise visits to her hairline, but she maintained radio silence.

Once my tale was spent, there was a moment of silent absorption. Polly took a lungful of scented air, letting it out in a long sigh. "W ell... that's a pretty packed taco," she finally said, eyebrows knitting together. After a beat, she let the hanging question loose. "Can you see a future with Jake, knowing all this?"

I studied my champagne, watching the bubbles frantically clawing their way to freedom. "Honest answer? I haven't a clue, Polly," I confessed. "Yes, Jake's been lying through his teeth. But then..." I bit my lip, trying to untangle the mess of my emotions. "There's a side of me that gets why he did what he did."

Polly was nodding, her expression far off. "Jake was on a justice mission," she noted. "There's something relatable there. But deceit always bites you in the rear, Lola. The real question is whether the two of you can weather the aftermath."

Polly was no oracle, but her words weighed heavy, echoing my own confused feelings. Hearts, unfortunately, aren't great at following reason.

Pivoting the conversation, Polly asked, "So, what's the game plan?" At least that was an easier question. "We go full disclosure with Harry," I answered, feeling a rush of resolve. "We lay out everything on the table and then we chart our way forward."

Polly breathed out, reclining in her chair, digesting the rollercoaster of information. "This mystery has more twists than a yoga class," she observed.

I laughed, taking a gulp of my champagne. "You could say that again."

Polly's eyes twinkled behind her cucumber mask. "Even with Jake's guilt-ridden confession, it doesn't all add up. Do you really believe they did all this, just the two of them?"

I faltered, swirling the champagne in my glass as I considered her point. Framing Marcella, planting phony evidence, staging a chase sequence that would make Spielberg proud...it all seemed a bit much, even for a man as desperate as Jake.

"So, you're suggesting there's a third musketeer?" I quirked an eyebrow at her.

Polly shrugged. "I don't know. But I think we should keep our eyes peeled for any curveballs and besides, from what you said, Jake never said he or Victor were responsible for the two murders we have on our hands."

Her words rang true. We were knee-deep in this mystery and couldn't afford any blind spots. "We'll have to go Sherlock on this," I concluded. "Turn this mystery inside out, follow the breadcrumbs again."

Polly nodded, her expression as sharp as a hawk's. "That's the least we owe the victims. Unraveling the whole truth, the no-nonsense, raw truth."

"Agreed," I said, raising my champagne flute. "To finding the truth, no matter how many spa days it takes."

With a chuckle, Polly clinked her glass against mine. "Amen to that. And to more spa days!"

As we lounged in our comfy spa chairs, bubbly water teasing our toes and thoughts bubbling at a similar pace, I felt the case tugging us back into reality. The spa was like an oasis of calm, offering temporary refuge, but our mystery was an impatient child, clamoring for attention. I eyed Polly, who mirrored my thoughts perfectly.

"I'd happily trade a quick resolution for an hour-long seaweed wrap," she remarked, her tone laced with a tinge of regret. "But I fear our mystery is getting antsy."

I concurred, reluctantly lifting my prune-like feet from the balmy water. "Should we take our detective hats to the Gallery Café then?"

She perked up, her eyes twinkling with renewed resolve. "Oh, absolutely. To the Gallery Café!"

With a reluctant farewell to our tranquil sanctuary, we found ourselves engulfed by the familiar scent of freshly brewed coffee.

Polly flumped into her seat across our regular café table, heaving an overly dramatic sigh. "Good heavens, this case is like trying to do a crossword puzzle with no vowels!"

I slid her mug of hot cocoa across the table. "Tell me about it. I'm starting to think we'll never solve this."

Polly took a sip of cocoa, smiling faintly. "Cheer up, grumpy pants. We've made it this far, haven't we?"

"Barely," I retorted. "Let's go over everything again. Maybe we missed a clue."

Polly nodded. "Alright, from the very beginning. Worthington's murder, the dagger Jake gave you."

"Which has now mysteriously disappeared."

"Don't forget Brittany," Polly said. "She admitted to having an affair with Worthington, giving her motive." I frowned. "But nothing proved she actually killed him."

Polly turned thoughtful. "Then there's Jake and Victor, sneaking around and paying each other off."

"Claiming they investigated Worthington for theft," I added.

"Yet they framed Marcella instead of coming clean," Polly pointed out.

"Which implies they aren't working alone," I said slowly.

Polly nodded. "They'd need help planting false evidence and chasing us." Polly began ticking off points on her fingers. "Jake said they had to plant false evidence to frame Marcella. And orchestrate that chase scene at the barn, which would have required help."

"You're right," I said slowly. "That does seem beyond what Jake and Victor could manage alone."

"But who benefits most if Marcella takes the fall?" I questioned.

Polly tapped her chin in thought. "The real killer!"

"Exactly!" I said excitedly. "So we need to analyze who gains the most with Marcella as the primary suspect."

"Time to pay Marcella another visit," Polly declared.

I nodded. "After talking to Harry about what we've found."

Polly lifted her mug. "To truth and justice. And pastries."

"Hear, hear!" I said, clinking my mug against hers. The case was far from solved, but at least now we had a fresh lead to pursue.

"Hold on," I said suddenly. "We're forgetting something - Brittany's murder."

Polly frowned. "You're right. That complicates things further."

"So we have two killers now," I mused. "One who murdered Worthington, and another who killed Brittany."

"With separate motives," Polly added.

I tapped my fingers on the table anxiously. "If Jake and Victor framed Marcella for Worthington's death, who killed Brittany?"

Polly looked uncertain. "I'm not sure. None of our suspects seemed to have anything against her…"

"This case just keeps getting more convoluted," I sighed in frustration.

"We'll figure it out, Lola. We always do."

"Maybe not this time, Pol."

As I locked the front door of the Gallery Café, I glanced back at the cozy interior, now shrouded in darkness. Tomorrow, we would confront Marcella, present our findings to Harry, and hopefully, get one step closer to solving this mystery.

Polly's voice broke through my thoughts. "Hey Lola, you coming?" She was waiting for me at the curb, her face illuminated by the soft glow of the streetlamp.

"Yeah, I'm coming," I replied, turning away from the café. As I walked away, I couldn't shake off a nagging feeling that we were missing something crucial. But what?

Chapter 29

"Still gives me the chills," Polly murmured as we stepped out of the car, the barn looming in the distance. Looking at the charred remains of the barn felt like being the guest of honor at a surprise party you knew about—uncomfortable and a little disappointing, with the vibrant green fields around mocking the poor, burned structure.

"Me too," I admitted, my mind flashing back to the day we'd narrowly escaped being run over. The world was just waking up, the quiet of the early morning punctuated by the distant crowing of a rooster. Yet, the tranquility of the dawn did little to soften the harsh reality of the blackened barn before us.

As we approached the barn, I noticed a figure moving amidst the ruins. A closer look revealed Marcella, her silhouette outlined against the soft morning light. She was arranging a small memorial for Brittany, her hands carefully placing flowers around a framed photograph. It was a poignant sight, a quiet tribute amidst the remnants of the past. We had received a tip from a local that Marcella had been visiting the barn every morning since Brittany's death, a ritual of remembrance for her lost cousin. Today was no different.

"Marcella," I called out, breaking the silence. She turned, her expression unreadable. "We need to talk."

"Lola, Polly," she greeted, her voice devoid of any warmth. Her eyes, however, told a different story. They were rimmed with red, the telltale sign of many shed tears. "I wasn't expecting to see you again."

Her words were casual, but there was a guardedness in her eyes that set off alarm bells in my head. Was she genuinely surprised to see us, or was this another act?

"We have some more questions," Polly said, her tone firm. "About Jake and Victor."

Marcella's eyes narrowed. "What about them?"

"We know they framed you," I said. "We want to know why."

"And why would I tell you?" Marcella retorted, her voice icy.

"Because we're trying to clear your name," I replied. "We believe you're innocent, Marcella. But we need your help to prove it."

She was silent for a moment, her eyes shifting between us. Then, with a sigh, she motioned for us to follow her. "Let's talk."

We followed her to a makeshift seating area, a couple of crates serving as chairs. As we sat down, I sighed and glanced around the barn. The place was eerily quiet, the only sound the crunch of our footsteps on the burned debris.

"Alright," Marcella said, crossing her arms over her chest. "What do you want to know?"

"Everything," Polly replied. "Start from the beginning."

Marcella hesitated, then began to speak.

"Very well," Marcella said, a hint of defiance in her voice. "As you know, Worthington's sudden death left me in quite a precarious position. His fortune and connections had helped fund my various charities and foundation work. So when the police started pointing fingers at me, I panicked."

"Victor and Jake approached me, claiming they had evidence that could exonerate me—if I helped them frame someone else instead. Like the fool I was, I agreed." Marcella's voice took on a bitter edge.

"Victor was like a demanding director, coercing me to plant breadcrumbs leading to Brittany. He even had me follow Brittany around, ensuring the press 'spotted' us in a dramatic argument, a real-life soap opera. I thought it would be enough to divert suspicion away from me." Her voice broke slightly at the mention of Brittany's name, a flicker of pain crossing her face. "I never ... I never thought it would lead to this. I loved Brittany. She was my family."

Marcella sighed. "But then Brittany was murdered too. And I realized Victor and Jake had been manipulating me from the very beginning. They needed a scapegoat for both murders." Her hand clenched into fists.

"When you two started snooping around, Victor warned me to stay away. But I refuse to be their silent accomplice any longer. If there's a way I can help clear my name and catch the real killer, I'll do it."

Marcella met our gazes, her expression fierce with determination. "I won't be made a fool of again. It's time those two answered for their crimes."

As she recounted her story, I found myself studying her. Her voice was steady, her face unwavering. But there was a certain tightness around her eyes, a subtle clenching of her jaw. Signs of stress, or guilt?

"We know about the theft," I said, interrupting her narrative. "Jake and Victor were investigating Worthington, weren't they?"

Marcella's eyes flickered, but she nodded. "Yes, they were."

"But they framed you instead of coming clean," Polly added. "Why?"

"I don't know," Marcella said, her voice barely a whisper. "I honestly don't."

"One more thing," I said, pulling the coins out of my pocket. "What are these? Are they stolen artifacts from the Johnston collection? We found these in the barn."

Marcella looked at the coins and then took them in her hand. She looked at them for a few moments. She seemed a bit puzzled and then suddenly a smile grew on her face. "No, no. They are not artifacts at all, or not ones with any real value. When I was younger, I loved treasures and old things like a pirate may have. I loved pirates. My father found these on one of his trips and brought them back to me. I used this barn as my 'ship'. I guess I just lost these in the barn, and there are probably more, but I have not thought about these in years."

I exchanged a glance with Polly. Marcella seemed sincere. But was she telling the truth? Or was she a better liar than we'd given her credit for?

"We're going to find out the truth about everything, Marcella," I said, my voice firm. "We're going to uncover whatever and whoever is behind all of this."

She met my eyes with a hard expression. "I hope you do, Lola. For the sake of everyone's sanity." Her words hung around us like a cryptic crossword puzzle. Polly and I exchanged a look. Marcella seemed to be on the up and up, but could we trust her, given her checkered resume in the deception department?

Chapter 30

Polly's fingers danced across her smartphone screen as we made our way down the driveway of Marcella's estate. "What are you doing?" I asked, my curiosity piqued.

"Texting Harry," she replied, her eyes never leaving the screen. "We need to fill him in on this latest development."

I nodded, my mind still reeling from Marcella's story. "You're right. Marcella's story may shed some light on this case, even if it doesn't fully exonerate her."

Polly hit send with a flourish and slipped her phone back into her pocket. "There, I've sent him a summary and told him we're on our way to the Gallery Café to discuss."

As we exited the gates, I was entrapped with a growing sense of unease. "Honestly, I'm not sure what to make of Marcella's story. She seems sincere, but she admitted to planting false clues."

Polly's face was thoughtful as I navigated the quiet country road. "We'll have to examine every part of her account closely. Look for inconsistencies, holes in her story."

"Easier said than done," I replied, my eyes drifting to the passing scenery. "Every new piece of information we uncover throws up more questions."

Harry was already at the café sitting in the booth he knew we reserved for ourselves, a monolithic presence with his granite expression and arms crossed like a fortress wall. The seriousness of his demeanor was such a contrast to the laid-back ambience of the café that I bit my tongue to stop from laughing. Talk about a cop in a coffee shop!

We slid into our customary booth, the air laced with the peculiar yet welcoming mix of warm cardamom-spiced cider and the vanilla-scented wax from hand-poured candles – an olfactory oxymoron to the grave discussion that was about to be served up. As we launched into our detailed recounting of Marcella's story, the clatter of cups and the buzz of the espresso machine offered a strangely soothing soundtrack.

Just as we were getting into the details, Thomas approached with a tray of coffee and pastries. "Good morning, ladies," he greeted, attempting to balance the tray as he navigated toward the table. In his earnestness to serve us, he misjudged the edge of the table, sending a cup of coffee toppling over. The hot liquid spread across the table, narrowly missing our notepads.

"Oh, I'm so sorry!" Thomas exclaimed, his face turning a shade of red that matched the café's brick walls. He hurriedly mopped up the mess with a handful of napkins, his movements only causing more chaos as a pastry followed the coffee's fate, landing with a soft plop onto Polly's lap.

Despite the situation, I let out a nervous laugh. Polly, ever the good sport, laughed it off and reassured Thomas that no harm was done, even though she did shoot me a "what on Earth are we going to do with him," look.

Once the table was cleaned and a fresh round of coffee served (this time successfully), we resumed our conversation. Harry listened intently, his eyes never leaving our faces. He occasionally interjected with a question or a request for clarification, his pen poised over his notepad.

When we finished, he was silent for a moment, his gaze distant as he mulled over our words. Finally, he spoke. "Marcella's version of events line up with what you witnessed of Jake and Victor's behavior." He tapped his pen against his notepad, a rhythmic sound that echoed my own racing heartbeat. "However, her story still has holes. If she framed Brittany for Worthington's murder, who killed Brittany?"

I frowned, Harry's words echoing my own thoughts. "And if Victor and Jake were targeting Worthington for theft, why kill Brittany at all?" Polly added, her voice laced with frustration.

Harry nodded, his gaze thoughtful. "Exactly. Two separate motives, two separate killers."

I sighed, the weight of our unsolved mystery pressing down on me. "So we're back to square one?"

Harry leaned back in the booth, his gaze steady on us. "It seems so. But remember, every piece of information, every story, brings us one step closer to the truth."

The conversation lulled as we contemplated this frustrating realization. After a few moments of silence, Polly glanced at her watch and sighed. "I have to head into the art store before lunch. Call me if anything new comes up?"

I nodded. "Of course. We'll keep digging and let you know if we find another lead."

Polly gathered her things and bid us farewell. An uneasy silence fell between Harry and me now that we were alone. His eyes met mine for just a second, a flicker of regret in those familiar blue eyes. I knew how invested I'd become in solving this mystery, how much was at stake - for the case, and for the fragile bond between us.

Harry cleared his throat, awkwardly breaking the silence. "How have you been holding up?" He gestured vaguely, unwilling or unable to give voice to the real question lingering in the air. "With all this—the case, Jake..."

His voice trailed into silence, but not before I noticed a green glint at the mention of Jake's name. He was jealous. I dropped my eyes to my coffee-stained apron, an echo of heartache bouncing around my chest. Jake and I were a mixtape of our younger years, but Harry had always been more of a classic rock kinda guy. Now, with Jake potentially being the bad guy in our real-life crime drama, things were messier than a toddler's birthday party.

Harry knew the tangled web of emotions between Jake and me. He also knew our heated argument, sparked by his dismissive attitude towards my detective prowess, still bothered me. He may as well have patted me on the head and sent me to go play with dolls. I had demanded his respect and trust, and his words had hurt more than a thousand paper cuts.

Just when I felt my insides folding into an origami of despair, Harry reached over and took my hand, his eyes mirroring the regret I had ached to see. "You know you can count on me, Lola," he said softly. "Anything you need, I'm here."

His words, so honest and raw, acted like a soothing lullaby to my stormy heart. I studied his face, its familiar lines reminding me of all the memories we shared, the laughter and the tears. Despite our clashes, Harry was my cozy blanket in this crazy, mixed-up world.

I squeezed his hand, a spark of hope fluttering within me like a defiant moth. "I know, Harry. Thank you." I hoped my eyes could express what my tongue couldn't—the depth of my need for his support to stitch together the trust we had ripped apart.

He looked softer, a glimmer of relief easing the tension etched onto his face. Maybe, just maybe, I could forgive him after all. "We should ... go back to the case," he suggested, but we remained rooted, savoring this delicate patch-up job more than the thrill of the hunt. After all, what was a mystery without a side of emotional drama?

Harry shifted, seeming unusually uncertain. "Listen, about what I said... dismissing you, that was wrong. You've shown me you're far more than 'just an amateur'. I was scared ... of putting you in danger. But that's no excuse."

His heartfelt confession stunned me, like a bunny caught in headlights. Yet, they echoed my own fears, our emotional vulnerabilities entwining like two strands of the same DNA.

I threw him a wry grin. "Well, I was scared too, you know. Scared that you didn't respect me ... didn't see me as your equal." A laugh bubbled up. "Guess we're both dummies, huh?"

Harry chuckled, a sound as comforting as my grandma's homemade chicken soup. "Certifiable dummies," he agreed, then sobered. "From now on, we're in this together. Mutual respect. Mutual trust. Deal?"

He extended his hand.

"Deal."

Chapter 31

Harry strolled by my side. The nocturnal symphony of Fawnwood was in full swing. We traipsed down its quaint, lantern-lit streets and the croaking frogs and nocturnal rustlings of Fawnwood's ever-observant wildlife. The delightful cottages that lined the way were asleep, their softly glowing windows suggesting residents cozied up with a cup of hot cocoa or a suspenseful mystery novel—likely the latter, given the recent town gossip. The subtle brushes of his hand against mine felt less like incidental contact and more like a Morse code of reassurance. Since our truce at the café, the tension between us had thawed. The icy wall of awkwardness was melting into a puddle, revealing the firm friendship we had before.

My eyes lifted to the velvet expanse above, dotted with a sequin-spray of stars. Their faithful patterns were like the steadfast old friends you'd call in the middle of the night. The Milky Way held her spiral arm out like an open highway, and Orion had his belt securely fastened, as usual, even if it did make him look a little like a celestial traffic cop.

"I've often thought," I mused aloud, my voice adding a layer to the night's chorus, "that Orion's belt is a bit tight. Don't you think? Might explain why he looks so grumpy."

Harry chuckled, a warm, low sound that matched the evening's tranquility. "Only you, Lola, would worry about the comfort of constellations."

That was the magic of Fawnwood, a place where even the tension of a murder mystery couldn't dampen our innate, quirky charm. Harry and I, two small town souls under the infinite sky, just trying to ensure the celestial bodies were at ease and the coffee kept flowing at the Gallery Café.

We walked on in comfortable silence until my apartment came into view, lights aglow in the windows. We made our way to the apartment door. As I fumbled for my key, Harry turned to me, his face half in shadow. "How is Tetley doing after his trip to the vet?"

I smiled, warmed by his thoughtfulness. "He's back to his usual carrot-crunching self. Dr. Mendel gave him a clean bill of health." My gaze drifted up to meet Harry's, finding those blue eyes watching me intently. "Thank you for asking ... it means a lot that you care about the little details."

Harry's expression softened. "I've always cared about the details when it comes to you, Lola."

A warmth blossomed in my chest at his words. Before I could form a response, a loud thump and crashing sound came from my apartment, followed by frantic scratching noises.

Harry and I hurried inside to investigate the source of the commotion. We rounded the corner of the entranceway to find Tetley scrambling in the confined space of his hutch, kicking up wood shavings in his panic to get free.

"The latch must have locked in place," I said, swiftly unhooking the hutch door. Tetley leaped out and into my waiting arms, his tiny heart racing under my fingers. I stroked his soft fur to soothe him as he burrowed into my embrace, his usual unflappable spirit shaken.

"It seems he's not quite recovered from his ordeal at the vet after all," Harry remarked, reaching over to gentle pet Tetley's head. Tetley sniffed Harry's hand in recognition, some of the tension leaving his small body at the familiar and comforting scents of home.

I cradled Tetley close, feeling his heartbeat slowly return to normal under my hands. "I think he just had a scare from being trapped. But he seems to be calming down now that he's free. He is not used to being locked in the hutch, just his carrier." I smiled up at Harry, gratitude shining in my eyes. "Thank you for being here. With everything that's been happening lately... I don't know what I'd do without you."

Tetley snuggled into my embrace, the frantic beat of his heart now a steady rhythm under my fingers. I smiled up at Harry, feeling lighter than I had in weeks. "I should put Tetley in his carrier for the night, so he feels secure. Will you wait here?"

Harry nodded, giving Tetley one last gentle pat. "Of course. Take your time."

I carried Tetley into the kitchen, reveling in the warmth of home. As I made my way, a giddy feeling bubbled up inside me. Here in the comforting familiarity of my home, with Tetley safe in my arms and Harry waiting just in the living room, everything felt right in a way it hadn't for so long.

Could it be that after the arguments and hurt, the dangers that had seemed determined to tear us apart, Harry and I were finding our way back to the beginning? The thought sent my heart racing with nervous hope.

I set Tetley in his carrier with a dish of his favorite berries to occupy him, then set about preparing tea in a happy daze. Two mugs, a blend of chamomile and mint, a splash of honey - little details came together to create a perfect moment.

As I waited for the kettle to boil, my eyes drifted around the cozy kitchen. How many times would Harry and I stand here together, laughing over a shared joke as we prepared a meal? The fantasy was bittersweet, highlighting all that might be if we were brave enough to rekindle the connection between us. A connection I feared lost, now tentatively peeking through the cracks to offer another chance.

The whistle of the kettle startled me out of my reverie. I prepared our tea with a smile and a silent wish—for new memories to be made here, possibilities reborn from the ashes of the past.

With one last glance around this space that held so many recollections of happiness, I made my way back into the living room where Harry waited. The two mugs I cradled close were a beginning, a promise of quiet moments to come. No longer divided by doubts and fears, but finding our way together again under familiar constellations, to create a new story of us. My heart swelled at the thought, spilling over with a joy I could hardly contain.

As I stepped back into the living room, I found Harry standing by the window, his expression altered in a way I couldn't quite decipher. The relaxed atmosphere from earlier seemed to have evaporated, replaced by an air of tension that settled over the room like a heavy fog.

"Harry?" I called out softly, confusion and worry flooding my voice. His gaze snapped to mine, and I was struck by the way his eyes, usually so warm and bright, now seemed dark and stormy. "What's wrong?"

He hesitated for a moment before rubbing the back of his neck and looking away, clearly struggling with his thoughts. The sight of him so distraught filled me with a sense of unease, as if the floor beneath me was suddenly unstable.

"Lola, I just received a phone call that's ... that's very concerning," he said, his voice strained with the effort to maintain composure. "It's about the Gallery Café."

The mugs in my hands suddenly felt heavy, as if weighted down by the gravity of Harry's words. I set the tea down on the coffee table, my heart pounding in my chest. "What happened at the café, Harry?"

Harry swallowed hard, his eyes darting back to the window before meeting mine again. "There was an anonymous tip. They found what appears to be a murder weapon—a bloody dagger—hidden under the floorboards. The evidence points to you, Lola."

I felt an icy shiver run down my spine, and my heart raced as the memories of that fateful day flooded back to me. I had hidden the dagger, but only to protect Jake, not because I had any part in the crime. "Harry, listen to me. I hid the dagger, but I didn't kill anyone. I was trying to help Jake, who was in trouble."

Harry's face was a mask of pain as he stood up and approached me. "I want to believe you, Lola, more than anything. But I have to do my job. You're under arrest."

Chapter 32

As I looked around the cell, I couldn't help but think that the interior decorator had truly outdone themselves in creating the most cliché jail experience possible. The damp, concrete walls sported an avant-garde array of peeling paint, while the dim light from the solitary bulb overhead provided just the right ambience for a cozy night in ... if your idea of cozy was a cold, unyielding cell.

I sat on the thin, worn mattress, which brought to mind those budget motels one might reluctantly stay at during a road trip, and pondered my current predicament. Granted, being arrested wasn't exactly on my bucket list, but it certainly added a touch of excitement to my otherwise mundane life.

As I idly traced a crack in the floor with my finger, I thought about Harry. I could still see the pained expression on his face as he had arrested me. The memory stung, but I couldn't help but believe that he still had faith in me. After all, we'd been through a lot together, and our friendship was stronger than a mere accusation.

The iron bars of the cell, while not exactly a design feature I'd choose for my own home, did offer an interesting view of the bustling police station outside. The comings and goings of officers and detainees provided a sort of makeshift reality TV show—"The Real Cellmates of Fawnwood," perhaps? It was no substitute for the comforting familiarity of my café, but it would have to do for now.

The occasional drip of water from a leaky pipe in the corner of the cell provided a rhythmic soundtrack to my thoughts as I considered my next move. I'd always been resourceful, and I wasn't about to let a little thing like being accused of murder dampen my spirits.

I was in the middle of brainstorming an escape plan involving a makeshift grappling hook and a daring leap across the hallway when I heard footsteps approaching. My heart raced with anticipation, and I looked up to see Harry standing outside my cell, his expression stern and his posture rigid.

"Lola," he said, his voice firm and professional. "We need to discuss a pressing matter."

I straightened up, my makeshift escape plan temporarily forgotten. "What is it, Harry? Have you found new evidence? Or maybe a witness who can vouch for me?"

He shook his head. "No, that's not it. I need to remind you that, regardless of whether you're guilty of murder, hiding a weapon is still a very serious offense. No matter what else, you would be charged with conspiracy to cover up a crime."

My eyes widened in surprise. "Whoopsies," I muttered, feeling a tinge of embarrassment. In the midst of trying to solve the case and clear my name, I hadn't considered the implications of my actions.

Harry's expression remained stern. "This isn't a joke, Lola.

Harry stood, his expression drawn as he stared at me. "You'll need a lawyer," he declared, with none of the warmth he'd shown earlier. The steely professionalism was back in full force. "I presume you don't have any in mind?"

"Lawyer?" I echoed, taken aback. Lawyers were creatures from television shows and movies, not characters I expected to be involved with. My mind raced. I'd never had to think about lawyers and trials before. My life had been about serving coffee, making small talk, and generally keeping the peace in Fawnwood. "Harry, I don't know any lawyers. I serve coffee, not subpoenas!"

Harry's mouth twitched at my response, a flicker of our shared humor shining through his stern façade. But it disappeared as quickly as it came. "You'll get a public defender then," he said, turning on his heel and making for the exit.

"Wait!" I called out, watching his retreating back. He paused, hand on the door, but didn't turn around. "Harry... do you believe me?"

The silence hung in the air, heavy with words unsaid. Finally, he spoke, his voice barely audible. "It's not about what I believe anymore, Lola." And with that, he walked out, leaving me alone with my thoughts and the cold reality of my predicament.

The moonbeam pierced through the barred window of my cell, splashing an ironic slice of cheer across the concrete floor. My heart wasn't in any sort of cheerful mood though. All I could think about was Harry, his words echoing in my mind. Was he really doubting me now? The thought stung, but I pushed it aside. There were bigger problems to face.

Namely, how on earth was I going to convince a public defender that I was innocent, especially when I'd been caught red-handed with hidden evidence? Boy, talk about dumb. How could I have been so stupid?

It was close to midnight when I heard the distinctive clatter of high heels echoing through the sterile hallway. The pace was lively, insistent even, and carried a rhythm that didn't belong to the usual wearers of the station's drab loafers. I peered through the iron bars, catching sight of a familiar pixie cut blonde hair rounding the corner.

"Polly?" I cried out, scrambling up from my cross-legged position on the hard cot.

Polly, was a vision amidst the gray drudgery of the police station. She was outfitted in her usual artistic flair, complete with a vibrant patchwork dress and a hat that could have doubled as a modern art installation.

"Lola!" she exclaimed, her grip tight on a handbag that matched her peacock-blue heels. "I heard and came running. You didn't think I'd leave you in here, did you?"

"Polly, you're a sight for sore eyes," I sighed, a wave of relief washing over me. Polly had been by my side through all the twists and turns of this mystery, and her presence now was an enormous comfort. "The situation's looking grim, isn't it?"

She gave a brisk nod, her normally jovial eyes serious. "It's the talk of the town, Lola, but we won't let this stain stick. You didn't do this, and we'll prove it."

Her unwavering faith in my innocence sent a surge of hope through me. We'd stumbled into this investigation together, and it was clear we'd see it through to the end, one way or another. "I need to get out of here, Polly, and clear my name."

"I know, Lola," she replied, the edges of her mouth twitching into her signature quirky smile. "And I've got your back. Plus, we have a great ally out there."

Feeling a spark of curiosity, I pressed, "Who?"

"Thomas, who else?" she chuckled. "He's manning the fort at the Gallery Café while you're ... um ... on vacation. He even attempted a latte art this morning, which turned out looking more like a potato than a heart, but he's trying."

Despite the dire circumstances, I sighed and shot her a wry smile. "Sounds like I'll be returning to quite a scene at the café."

Though Polly tried to get me out, I ended up spending the night in this lovely facility. The next morning, the guard on duty brought me a very interesting-looking breakfast. One, I didn't think I couldn't keep down with the way my stomach already felt.

The interrogation room was as welcoming as a dentist's chair - bare walls, a one-way mirrored window, and a metal table coupled with two seats that could easily double as torture devices. My stomach churned with anxiety. I felt I had done nothing wrong and yet found myself here once more.

The door opened and Harry walked in, a file folder in hand. His expression was unreadable. I longed for a glimpse of our familiar ca-maraderie, but understood he had a job to do.

He settled across from me, making the chair groan in protest. "Lola, I know you're innocent of murder. But I need your help to prove it. And if we can do that, maybe we can somehow get you out of being charged with conspiracy."

A tide of relief swept over me, and I stared straight at him. "Just tell me what to do, Harry."

Harry opened the folder, revealing photos of the crime scene. "Walk me through everything that happened the night of the masquerade ball."

Taking a deep breath, I recounted our discovery of Worthington's body, our initial suspect of Victor, Jake approaching me about hiding the dagger and what he had said about it proving 'his' innocence. My story came spilling out in tangles, explanations mixed with apologies. Harry listened intently, piecing together the fragments.

When I finished my recounting, Harry shuffled through the photos, pausing on one. He sighed and pinched the bridge of his nose. "Lola, I have some troubling news regarding Brittany's murder."

My heart sank. "What is it, Harry?"

He met my gaze, his eyes dark with worry. "The initial autopsy report came back. Brittany was killed with the same type of weapon as Worthington—a ceremonial dagger."

I gasped. "The same dagger? But that would mean..." My voice trailed off as the horrifying reality settled over me. There wasn't a set of individual murderers for each victim, as we'd initially thought. Instead, there was a single, cold-blooded killer.

Harry nodded grimly. "It seems the dagger you hid at the café was the murder weapon for both victims."

I swallowed hard, my mind reeling. The implications were devastating. "You think Jake used me to hide the murder weapon?"

"It's a possibility we can't ignore," Harry said. "If Jake is guilty, I need you to tell me, Lola. Hiding evidence to protect someone makes you an accessory."

I fought back tears, my world spinning. Had Jake manipulated me from the start? The man I thought I knew now seemed a stranger wearing his face.

Harry's words cut through my thoughts. "Lola, I need the truth. Now." His voice hardened with authority, professional detachment replacing our usual rapport. The change stung, a reminder of how much was at stake.

I met his eyes, steeling my resolve. "Jake may have lied to me, I don't know, but he never said he killed anyone, just that the dagger might help prove him innocent. I won't help frame an innocent man. I know I should have handed the dagger over to you, Harry. I know I shouldn't have ever touched it in the first place. I have screwed up some things, but I murdered no one."

Harry studied me for a long moment before nodding. "I believe you." His expression softened. "We'll find another way."

Chapter 33

A fresh-faced public defender named Marcus eventually arrived, looking more like a grad student than a seasoned lawyer. With a stack of legal documents under one arm and a cup of high-octane coffee in the other, he explained that Harry had found a new lead, creating reasonable doubt around my case.

"I know it's not ideal, Lola," Marcus said, the earnestness in his young eyes doing little to reassure me. "But it's enough to get you out of here. The investigation is ongoing, so I need you to stick around town, okay? And try to keep a low profile."

With a shake of his head and a last sip of his coffee, Marcus promised to meet me at the café to go over the specifics. When he was done, I was escorted back to my cell to gather my things—what few there were—and released, my exit from the jail as unceremonious as my entrance had been.

The morning was still fresh when I stepped outside the station, the world rushing back in a whirl of color and noise. Freedom, as it turned out, smelled like car exhaust and freshly brewed coffee from the café down the street. Harry had come to see me out, his face etched with concern.

"Lola, remember we're not out of the woods yet. The case is still open." His tone was grave, his warning clear. I nodded, squinting in the morning sun. But, for a moment at least, I was free.

The Gallery Café was bustling with its usual assortment of chatter and clinking crockery when I entered. Amidst the crowds of patrons, Thomas stood behind the counter in his element—having left his clumsy nature behind for a morning, miraculously not causing any disasters.

Upon spotting us, his face split into a wide grin. "Lola, you're free!" he cried, darting from behind his station to wrap me in an enthusiastic hug, his apron dusted with coffee grounds and splashes of milk.

"I was starting to think I'd have to run this place permanently!" His mock dismay couldn't hide the relief in his voice. I chuckled, patting his back.

"Then you'd have to deal with all the paperwork, Thomas. Trust me, you'd miss the coffee spills."

His laughter rang out, easing the tension still knotted in my chest. He shook his head, returning to his post to manage the growing queue of customers.

Before I could fully absorb the relief of being back, a whirlwind in the form of Polly barreled towards our booth. Her vibrant hair—a blonde that would put the midday sun to shame—fanned out around her, and her smock sported fresh daubs of paint.

"Lola, you're back!" She exclaimed, her arms finding their way around me in a comforting squeeze. "I tried everything I could last night. I am so sorry. We have been worried sick! I mean, Thomas here almost burned the espresso machine out of sheer worry!" She gave a playful wink towards Thomas, who feigned indignation.

Settling into the worn leather of our regular booth, I nodded. "It's good to be back, Polly."

Over steaming mugs of coffee, I relayed the conversations and events I'd had at the station. My narrative echoed in the cozy space of our booth. Their expressions mirrored each other—shock, confusion, then dawning comprehension.

Polly exhaled sharply, setting her mug down with a thud. "So, Jake lied about the dagger all along. He used it, then had you stash it." Her voice held an edge, hard as her cerulean gaze.

I nodded, the bitterness of betrayal seeping into my words. "It's hard to believe, but ... it all seems to point that way."

"At least your name will be cleared," Polly said with a grin. "That's the most important thing."

I had barely finished speaking when the door to the café swung open with a clatter, drawing all eyes to the new arrival. In the doorway stood Marcus, his face pale even under the café's warm lighting. He looked shaken, his hand gripping a folder tightly.

"I... I have bad news," he stammered, making his way to our table. The room fell silent, the clinking of cutlery and hum of conversation fading into a nervous hush. "There's been a development. Lola, they've ... they've found additional evidence."

His words landed like a punch. The fresh air of freedom I had been breathing only moments ago suddenly felt heavy, a noose tightening once again around my neck.

"What... What kind of evidence?" I choked out.

His eyes met mine, a deep apology dwelling in their depths.

"We need to talk," he said grimly. "In private."

We went into the back office that I rarely used and shut the door. "The new evidence," he began, as his eyes darted over my face, like he was searching me for a reaction, "it's a jacket ... found near the crime scene. It has traces of the victim's blood on it. They've tested it. The DNA is a match." I swallowed hard, my mind racing. "And the jacket?"

"Lola, the police think it is yours." He paused, drawing a shaky breath. "It's a jacket from the café. Your café."

"Polly and I didn't wear our jackets to the Fawnwood Museum event..." I tried to say before he interrupted me.

"Lola, the worst part... the inside tag has a staff name."

His words hung in the air, their implication slowly sinking in. My mind raced through the list of people it could be, a sickening sensation bubbling in my gut. "Who?" I managed to choke out. "Mine?"

"We don't know for sure yet. The tag is smudged, partially torn ... it's hard to tell. The only letter that can be made out is an 'a'." He took a deep breath, steadying himself, "Just promise me you'll be careful, okay? Trust no one until we figure this out."

Before I could press him further, a voice interrupted us as the door swung open. "Lola! There you are!" It was Thomas, his face flushed from the morning rush, his eyes darting between me and Marcus with a flicker of ... was it worry? Or something else? "Lola, the customers are asking for you. We really need your help out here." His tone was casual, but there was an urgency in his voice that felt out of place. Caught off guard, I merely nodded, giving Marcus a questioning look.

"We'll continue this later, okay?" Marcus said, casting a glance towards Thomas before walking away.

Chapter 34

B y lunchtime, the café was humming with the rhythm of the midday rush. It felt good to be back, to be a part of the life I had known before my world was upended. Yet, as I glanced across the room, my eyes falling on Thomas's unusually serene demeanor, something gnawed at me. A question, an anomaly that needed exploring.

The usually clumsy Thomas was now deftly managing the crowd. Over the past week, I had observed subtle changes in his demeanor, his efficiency improving, the accidents suddenly less frequent. The transformation was startling, honestly, making me reconsider the events of the past few days.

His early arrival at the café the day the dagger went missing, his peculiar eagerness to help, the traces of worry, or perhaps guilt, in his eyes when Marcus entered the café saying he had bad news, saying they had found new evidence. All these pieces formed an unsettling image.

Polly's touch on my arm startled me and snapped me out of my thoughts. Her cerulean eyes were filled with worry as she searched my face. "You okay, Lola?" Her voice was a low whisper, just loud enough for me to hear over the café's buzz.

I attempted to brush off her concern with a shaky smile, "Just a little tired, that's all." She looked skeptical but didn't push further.

The rest of the day passed in a blur. Polly headed out to teach her art class. As the last patrons trickled out and Thomas and I were left alone, the deafening silence of the café felt oppressive. Thomas was still busily cleaning behind the counter, his back to me.

Taking a deep breath, I approached him. "Thomas," I started, my voice wavering slightly. "We need to talk."

He turned around, his brows knitted in confusion. "Sure, Lola. What's up?"

Taking another steadying breath, I plunged into my inquiry. "Did you work at the museum, Thomas?"

His movements stilled, his eyes widening just a fraction before he composed himself. "Yes, I did. Why do you ask?" The casualness in his voice didn't fool me. I noted the flicker of something that passed through his eyes—a hint of surprise? Guilt?

I swallowed hard. How could I have missed that when he was hired? Did I just not pay attention because we needed the help? "Were you fired from the museum?" The question hung in the air, thick and stifling.

Thomas froze. His face paled, his mouth opening and closing as he grappled for words. His reaction was confirmation enough, a sudden chill running down my spine. A lump formed in my throat as I stepped back, suddenly feeling as if the air had been sucked out of the room.

A million thoughts raced through my mind. Thomas, the sweet, clumsy, slightly incompetent barista, entangled in this horrid mess. The implications of this new revelation were daunting, the puzzle pieces starting to form a terrifying picture.

The café was eerily quiet as I walked out, leaving a stunned Thomas behind.

The biting wind stung my cheeks as I raced through the streets, my mind churning with Thomas's revelation. He had been fired from the museum; he started working for me shortly before Worthington was killed. It was just a coincidence, wasn't it?

With a sense of urgency nipping at my heels, I arrived at the imposing edifice of the Fawnwood Museum. Its grandeur felt mocking, hiding sordid secrets behind its refined façade. I took a moment to steady myself before pushing through the colossal oak doors, praying Victor and Jake could provide the clarity I so desperately needed.

Inside, the museum echoed with a silence that sent a shiver down my spine. The usually bustling grand halls stood empty, save for the timeless artifacts peering down from their pedestals. It felt eerie, almost foreboding.

Navigating the vast labyrinth of exhibits, I reached Victor's office, its seclusion feeling ominous. I knocked lightly, the sound ringing out in the silence. The door creaked open at Victor's call, revealing his surprised face.

"Lola," he uttered, rising from his chair, shock lining his features. "What brings you here?"

Unable to find a gentler way to broach the topic, I blurted, "Thomas." I paused, taking a shaky breath before continuing, "I found out he used to work here."

Victor exhaled slowly, sinking back into his chair. He glanced over at Jake, who I had not seen standing in the corner until now. "Yes,

Thomas worked here," he admitted, looking more aged than I'd ever seen him. "He was ... let go."

"Fired, you mean," I corrected, bitterness creeping into my tone.

He nodded reluctantly, casting a worried glance at Jake. "It was... complicated, Lola."

"Was it?" I shot back, irritation prickling at my nerves. "Why was Thomas fired, Victor?"

He sighed heavily, the weight of the secret seeming to physically burden him. "It was Worthington's decision. There were discrepancies ... artifacts went missing under Thomas's watch. Some daggers and another piece or two from the Johnston collection. Despite his claims of innocence, Worthington ... had no choice."

The room seemed to spin around me. Discrepancies? Missing artifacts? The image of Thomas, the clumsy, good-natured barista, was crumbling, revealing a dangerous potential suspect in its place.

"Discrepancies," I echoed, forcing myself to remain calm. "And now, artifacts from this museum are at the center of two murder investigations."

Jake finally stepped forward, his deep voice barely above a whisper. "We didn't think Thomas had anything to do with any of this, Lola. We really didn't. He had already found a new job...at the Café. But the stolen daggers, well when you found one of them with blood on it, I was afraid I would be a suspect, but if they found who stole the daggers, it might clear my name if necessary."

Chapter 35

I left Victor's office in a daze, the weight of the revelation pressing heavily on my chest. My mind spun as I wandered through the museum halls, passing by priceless artifacts without truly seeing them. Thomas had been fired from the museum, and now, the reality of what that might mean cast a chilling shadow over everything I thought I knew about him.

Before I knew it, I had meandered into the exhibition hall, the room where it had all started - the charity ball, the murder, and the stolen dagger. Jake had followed me, his steady presence a quiet reassurance in the swirling storm of my thoughts.

As we stood there, wrapped in silence, the distant sound of a door creaking open sent a chill down my spine. Someone else was in the museum. Jake stiffened beside me, his hand instinctively moving to the small security radio at his belt. But before he could make a call, a familiar voice echoed through the hall, freezing us both in our tracks.

"Jake, Lola," called Thomas, his voice chillingly casual. He emerged from the shadows, an eerie smile playing on his lips. "Fancy seeing you here."

"Why, Thomas?" I heard myself ask, my voice sounding distant. "Why did you do it?"

Thomas shrugged, his eyes steady on us. "It's simple, Lola. Worthington treated me like dirt. I gave years of my life to this museum, lived and breathed these artifacts, and how did he repay me? He fired me on a whim over a false accusation."

Thomas's face hardened, bitterness etching deep lines across his features. "Worthington took everything from me. My passion, my purpose ... he crushed it without a second thought. And why?" Thomas let out a mirthless laugh. "Because he could."

Thomas began pacing, his voice rising in anger. "After devoting myself to that tyrannical bastard all those years, enduring his insults and demands, you want to know why I did it? Revenge. Worthington deserved to suffer for how miserably he treated me. For once, I wanted him to feel as powerless as he made me feel, every single day I worked under him."

A realization hit me as he spoke, stopping me in my tracks. "It wasn't a false accusation. It was you. You stole the Johnson artifact, didn't you?"

Thomas froze, his confident expression faltering. His eyes flicked away from mine, and he swallowed hard. "I... I don't know what you're talking about."

"Don't lie to me!" I shouted. "Brittany's list - one item was crossed out. It was you. Admit it!"

Thomas stood up a little taller, his anger rising. "Alright, you win," He seethed. "Yes, I stole it. I hid it under the floorboards of your precious café." His lips twisted into a sinister smile. "You hired a thief without even realizing it."

Thomas came to a stop, an unsettling calmness coming over his features. "When the opportunity arose to steal from the museum, to take back some small measure of power, I couldn't resist. And then, at the gala, I had my opportunity... No one knew I was there, and I slipped in as one of the café staff."

His lips twisted into a sinister smile. "The look of shock and fear on Worthington's face in that last moment made all the years of abuse worthwhile."

"And Brittany?" I asked, my voice barely above a whisper. "Why is she dead?"

"Brittany..." Thomas paused, his smile faltering. "Poor Brittany. She should have stayed out of it."

"Out of what?" I demanded, my voice echoing in the empty hall.

"Brittany found out. She came to the café that day to confront me. She'd connected the dots about the missing artifact."

"Or maybe she wanted to find evidence," Jake interjected, his eyes never leaving Thomas. "Is that why you killed her, Thomas? To silence her?"

For a moment, Thomas didn't answer. Then he let out a slow sigh, his shoulders slumping. "I couldn't have her running to the police, could I?" He gulped. "Luckily, I had the perfect murder weapon right there. The same dagger that killed her lover, and you were the one to bring it to me, Lola."

The room spun around me as the pieces fell into place. Thomas, the thief and the murderer, had been hiding in plain sight all along.

Thomas's eyes suddenly darkened toward me, a spark of renewed rage flashing in their depths. "And you're no different, are you?" he spat, beginning to advance on me. "Taking over the café from your uncle, acting as if you care—but you're just the same as everyone else. You'll use me, berate me, throw me aside once you have what you want!"

I stumbled back, stunned by the vehemence in his words. "Thomas, no, I would never..."

He cut me off with a menacing glare. "LIAR!" he shrieked. "You're all the same—taking advantage of me, wanting me gone once I've outlived my purpose!"

Thomas's outburst rang in my ears, his unbridled rage rendering me momentarily speechless. Before I could find my voice, he lunged at Jake, a sharp object glinting ominously in his hand.

His eyes were wild, mouth twisted into a sinister snarl as he swung the weapon. I gasped, stumbling back as my heart leaped into my throat. Jake narrowly dodged the blow, the blade missing by inches. The roar escaping Thomas's lips turned my blood to ice.

They grappled, shadows stretching ominously across the grand hall. Thomas had height and sheer madness on his side, but Jake matched him for strength. As they struggled, kicking up debris in their furious fight, I scrambled for anything that could help. My trembling hands closed around a harmless but weighty replica spear from a display case filled with replica artifacts for kids to interact with.

With a cry, I swung the weapon, the blunt tip hitting Thomas's arm. He roared in pain, releasing Jake and turning his furious face toward me. I swung again with all my might. He fell to the floor and let out an unearthly howl. He had fire in his eyes. His rage seemed barely human; teeth bared like a wild animal, he lunged toward me.

Before I could react, Jake lunged at Thomas, tackling him to the floor as if he was a linebacker. Thomas's eyes were wild, mouth twisted into a sinister snarl as he swung the weapon in rage and desperation. I gasped, stumbling back as my heart leaped into my throat. Jake evaded the blow once again, the blade flung from Thomas's hands. Thomas bolted toward a back exit but stopped in his tracks as a swarm of uniformed officers, weapons drawn, emerged from the door.

Thomas turned and ran toward the front exit. In his haste, he passed close to where Jake was still kneeling on the floor. Jake dove in front of Thomas. Thomas fell to the floor face first with a loud thud.

Harry seemed to come out of nowhere. He pinned Thomas to the floor while he put the handcuffs on him. As he stood Thomas up, he handed him over to the officer standing next to them. "Read him his rights, and get him out of here."

"We got him, Lola," Harry murmured, his voice barely audible over the commotion. "It's over."

I let out a shaky breath, the truth of his words sinking in. After the whirlwind of danger and revelations, I couldn't believe the murderer was finally caught, and even harder to believe, it was Thomas.

I gave Harry an enormous hug. He gave me a soft smile. "I told you I would always have your back. And don't worry. I think we can now take care of your arrest situation with not too much trouble." After taking our statements, and Victor's, who we figured out was the one to call the police, Harry left to return to the police station.

The night wasn't quite over with yet. A nagging thought kept playing in my mind. I turned to Jake. "There's something we have to do."

Under the cover of night, we headed into the Gallery Café. I pulled up the loose floorboards behind the counter and saw nothing but empty space. Jake pried up several more surrounding floorboards with a crowbar in hand. After a few planks were removed, a glint of gold caught the dim light.

Jake let out a low whistle. "You were right."

He reached down, lifting a dazzling gold and emerald artifact from its hiding place. The missing Johnston piece, more valuable than Thomas had realized. I shook my head in disbelief that the treasure had been under our noses the whole time.

Jake turned to me, the artifact glittering in his hands, a roguish grin on his face. "Does this mean the case is officially solved, detective?"

I laughed, the threat of the past weeks finally losing its grip. The café felt warm and welcoming again. "I believe so. Now, how about a celebratory slice of cherry pie? I think we've earned it."

Jake slipped an arm around me, pulling me close with a contented sigh. "Cherry pie and your delightful company? I can't imagine anything better."

Epilogue:

Two months later...

The familiar strains of a string quartet drifted through the Gallery Café, echoing the music from that fateful night months ago when my world was first turned upside down. Masquerade Mondays had become a weekly tradition, in honor of new beginnings. Now as I watched couples swaying and twirling on the dance floor in their glittering masks, a sense of peace washed over me.

Polly glided up, wearing a frothy pink confection that matched her bubbly personality. She flashed me a thumbs up and an impish smile. "There's an adoring public waiting for your famous chocolate croissants, as well as your new charming barista."

I shook my head, chuckling. Some things never changed. "Coming right up."

As I headed to the kitchen, memories of that masquerade ball flickered through my mind like shadows, their power to haunt me diminishing day by day. While the journey had been harrowing, I realized every twisting turn led me to this moment. And for the chance to begin anew, I would travel its winding path again.

In the kitchen, Jake was slicing fruit for the salads, the apron he wore bringing back another memory, less somber. My heart gave a little flutter at the warmth in his eyes when he glanced up. "Need some help?"

I reached for his hand, giving it a squeeze. "I always do." So much had shifted since that first uncertain date. While the truth had taken its time emerging from the in-between spaces where it hid, Jake's heart, for me, remained a constant.

We worked side by side in a companionable rhythm, stealing kisses and feeding each other bites of juicy strawberries and flaky croissants. A familiar figure strolled through the doors then, bringing another reminder of how lives intersect in the most unlikely ways.

"The usual, Marcella?" I asked.

She nodded, smiling warmly. "And a croissant, if you please. Victor will be joining me today."

After Thomas's crimes and the tangled web of truths they revealed, Marcella and Victor had emerged as unlikely allies. While past betrayals lingered, their rediscovered friendship was a reminder that even rivalries couldn't withstand the test of time.

"On the house," I said, adding an extra croissant to her tray.

Marcella's eyes twinkled. "Oh, and do ask that charming detective of ours to come in, won't you?"

I glanced outside to where Harry waited, watching the crowd with a wistful air, hands folded behind his back. I glimpsed a flicker of longing in his eyes and knew in that moment, my heart would always remain torn between what was, and what might have been.

Jake followed my eyes, giving my hand a squeeze. "Will you invite our friend to join us?"

"Of course," I said softly.

While Thomas could never undo the harm, each life lost would be remembered. And in forging new bonds of trust, their memories were honored.

We watched as Harry made his way to Victor and Marcella, launching into animated conversation. Before long, they were swapping stories and sharing laughter, croissant crumbs and super-foam mustaches momentarily forgotten.

Polly breezed by, coffees and fresh pastries in hand, tossing a playful wink over her shoulder. I stifled a giggle as Jake's mask slipped sideways, revealing half of that irresistible crooked smile. Some masks were meant to come off, in time.

Epilogue

An epilogue is very similar to a prologue, but it occurs at the end of your story, though usually separate from the main plot. It might offer a glimpse of the future to share a sense of closure with your readers, or entice them to read the next in a series or collection.

Similar to the prologue, the epilogue should be placed in the main body content of your book and is therefore not technically back matter.

Also By Sydney Tate

About the Author

Sydney Tate has lived in North Carolina her entire life, but has lived in both the mountains and near the ocean. She has been a special education teacher for 27 years, a job she has always been passionate about. Sydney lives with her son, 3 cats, and a very large dog. In her free time, Sydney enjoys working in the yard, hiking, camping, kayaking, easy mountain biking, playing card and board games, and spending time with family and friends. She also enjoys watching football and hockey. Her favorite movie is Beaches, favorite TV show is M*A*S*H and favorite book series is Lord of the Rings. Some of her other favorite authors are Terry Brooks, Sue Grafton, and Rita Mae Brown.

https://www.facebook.com/sydneytatemysteries

Twitter sydneytatemys

Instagram sydneytatemysteries

www.ingramcontent.com/pod-product-compliance
Lightning Source LLC
Chambersburg PA
CBHW021156160726
47994CB00001B/230